SpyGirls Press
P.O. Box 1537
Fairfax, VA 22038
Visit our website at www.spygirlspress.com

First Edition: October 2013

The characters and events portrayed in this book are
fictitious. Any similarity to real persons, living or dead, is
coincidental and not intended by the authors.

Library of Congress Cataloging-in-Publication Data
Mahle, Melissa and Dennis, Kathryn
Camp Secret/Melissa Mahle and Kathryn Dennis,
Illustration by Liz Wong

1st ed. P. cm. – (Junior Spies Series, Book 1)
Summary: Under the cover of a deceptively normal summer
camp, a select group of recruits face weeks of training, mind
games and betrayal in a top secret Junior Spy program.

ISBN – 978-0-9852273-4-0
[1. Action & Adventure – Fiction.
2. Mysteries & Detective – Fiction.]
Library of Congress Control Number: 2013908320

Acknowledgments

We'd like to thank our teen readers who gave us the type of critiques authors really need: honest, teen-centric, and highly creative (it would be cool if…): Hana Mahle, Katie Watson, Charlie Flynn, and Frannie Vonada

A special thanks to Sylvia Whitman, Laska Hurley, Chris Boutee, and Joani Benoit.

To our editor, Kim Hamilton who questioned everything and double-checked it twice and Bruce Williams for his keen eye.

Last but not least, to our families for their support.

Also from SpyGirls Press
Lost in Petra (An Anatolia Steppe Mystery)
☆ "The Anatolia Steppe Mysteries series debuts with this craftily plotted novel crammed with mistaken identities, false leads, enigmatic clues, and narrow escapes."
Publishers Weekly Select, starred review

www.spygirlspress.com

CAMP SECRET

by
Melissa Mahle & Kathryn Dennis

This material has been reviewed
by the CIA to prevent the disclosure
of classified information.
(really)

spygirlspress

Contents

1

The Deception Begins

At first glance, Camp International looked almost normal. Buried deep in the woods of Virginia, it might have been mistaken for any of a dozen teen summer camps in the area. To the untrained eye, that is.

If the campers arriving on this particular Friday paid attention, they might have noticed that the cardinal sitting above their heads did not chirp or sing. Or the rock several of them tripped over while leaving the bus wasn't really granite, but lightweight polyurethane. Bolted to the ground, the concealment device hid a sensor that gave each arrival a full body-scan. If any of them bothered to look past the leaves skipping by their feet, they would have realized some of the trees did not move in the wind. But then, a great deal of effort had gone into making sure no one would notice, not even Lee Wong, the best watcher among them.

Lee did notice the departure of the buses with 98 percent dread, two percent curiosity. As the last bus left the parking lot, two metal gates slid across the opening, cutting off access to the outside world. A man dressed in camouflage pants and a green T-shirt and carrying a large chain emerged from a shack next to the gate. He wrapped the chain around the posts and secured it with an odd-looking lock with five push buttons instead of a dial.

While the other campers picked up their nametags and bunk assignments, Lee continued to watch. The gate secured, the guard walked to an electrical panel mounted on the side of the shack. He flipped a switch. Out of the ground rose a metal barrier and spikes. Lee studied them. Even if the gate were open, no car could leave the area without losing all four tires and most likely its entire underside, unless maybe it was one of those gigantic trucks from his favorite video game, *Monster Madness*. The man hit a second switch and a light on the panel turned from green to red. Lee studied the gate. Other than the light change, he couldn't see what the switch did. Green to red? On to off? Or safe to danger?

Loudspeakers blared overhead, calling the campers to the mess hall for the official opening of Camp International. At the mere suggestion of food, Lee's stomach rumbled at full volume. If it wasn't for the chaos and noise around him, Lee was certain everyone would have heard it. His hands reached for his belly—a second before he found himself on the ground, his mouth full of dirt.

A sturdy boy with two oversized duffle bags smiled down at him. The boy was about Lee's age, 13, or maybe 14. He wore a faded leather jacket despite the humid weather and black cowboy boots, and he had a thick head of sandy blond hair.

"Sorry dude," he said with a distinctive Texas drawl. "I gotta watch where I'm going." He dropped one of the duffels and gave Lee a hand. "My name's Tex. Tex Shaker."

Lee brushed the dirt out of his dark hair, which poked out in all directions in Tex's reflective sunglasses. "Lee Wong," he said, jabbing his finger at the gritty nametag stuck to the front of his shirt. But the boy and the duffels were on the move. Lee didn't even have the chance to explain this was his fault, that he had an unfortunate habit of being in the way.

He trailed behind the leather jacket like a lab rat following a piece of cheese. If he stayed close, maybe some of the cool would rub off on him. He needed some SWAG, according to his brothers. Something We Asians Got. Even his brothers made fun of his bulky frame, which made his head look too small and his hair a startled afterthought. His thick glasses magnified his black eyes to bug-like orbs.

His parents had been talking up this camp for the past year despite Lee's insistence that he was perfectly happy with his life. He didn't need to be "exposed" to new influences. Every day in the lab was a day of discovery. He did not want to go to camp even if the brochure said it was the top hands-on science programs in the nation.

The real problem was his dad. He thought Lee spent too much time holed up by himself. He knew his dad wanted him to be more like his brothers—sports champions and popular. Lee was a total failure at all things athletic. Perhaps he should be happy his dad hadn't sent him to wrestling camp. The thought of being grabbed by someone and thrown to the ground and twisted into unnatural positions made Lee shudder. Yep, it definitely could be worse.

Lee stood at the entrance of a whitewashed, wood-plank building after Tex dropped his bags and went in. There was no sign over the door, but as the smell of tomatoes, basil and garlic wafted toward him; he knew he had found the mess hall. A second sniff suggested meatballs. Lee was already salivating when he finally stepped inside. Tex had disappeared into the cavernous space. Lee's hope of making friends with fellow scientific minds faded as he studied the chaos in front of him.

The shouting started in the food line. A boy with short, dark hair and knobby knees poking out below soccer shorts tried to cut to the front of the line. Two boys ejected him.

Lee couldn't see who threw the first punch, but the fight was on. It was like a huge magnet, drawing in boys, including the one in the leather jacket. Lee held onto the door and dug his fingernails into the wood in case the magnetic pull turned his direction.

Then the food started flying. Lee ducked to avoid slices of garlic bread, which bounced off the wall behind him. A supersized portion of spaghetti splattered against a girl, turning her white blouse red, matching her ponytail and flushed face. Her tears left streaks through the sauce as a second wave of pasta hit. The girl looked at Lee and yelled something Lee could not understand over the taunts and screams.

"Save the spaghetti," Lee yelled back. It was his favorite, and the sight of it being wasted before he could get some made his stomach roar even louder.

The girl must have misheard him because she started toward him, but slipped, taking down a camp counselor. Eyeing the growing pile of arms and legs wrestling on the floor between him and the pasta, Lee calculated the odds of reaching the pot before it was too late.

As he let go of the door, a force field of a different kind hit the campers. A woman at least six feet tall stood on the raised podium in front of them, her sharp, angled face motionless. Her pale blue eyes pierced the room, daring anyone to move another millimeter.

"ENOUGH!" the woman shouted. Her voice had the edge of a drill sergeant.

Words froze on lips, and even the food seemed to stop mid-air as the commanding voice ended the free-for-all. "I wanted to welcome you to Camp International, but I am beginning to have my doubts about all of you. Food-fights, fistfights and the behavior I have witnessed tonight are a first for this camp. I expect each of you to start cleaning."

A girl with a mass of dark ringlets dropped to her knees scooping gobs of green beans off the floor, grumbling that she was not going to be sent home because of a bunch of stupid boys. The girl splattered with spaghetti joined her, and soon the other campers were sweeping away the spent ammunition. Lee recovered the garlic bread slices and shoved them into the pocket of his cargo shorts. He could not bring himself to throw good food away.

When the room fell silent again, the woman continued in such an icy tone that Lee double-checked to see if her hair just looked white, or was actually covered with frost.

"I only hope the counselors, many now covered in food, will be treated with the respect they deserve over the next eight weeks. I'm Ms. Markum, your camp director. I will now turn the floor over to Mr. Corwin, who will be overseeing your daily classes and programs."

Mr. Corwin bounded onto the stage to join Ms. Markum. It was so quiet Lee could once again hear his stomach complain. The man with wire-framed glasses and bushy red hair reminded Lee of a clown. He wore a fat tie decorated with red and green jellybeans. Lee liked him instantly. Eyes on the platform, Lee inched his way toward the food line, hoping the funny-looking guy would hold everyone's attention long enough for him to score the last of the spaghetti.

"Welcome to each of our 100 campers coming from 48 different states, many with multi-cultural backgrounds. Tomorrow you will begin with aptitude tests," Mr. Corwin announced. "We will use the tests to learn more about your interests, as well as any special skills each of you might possess. Attitude and aptitude are the keys to your success here. I will see you in the morning."

"Thank you, Mr. Corwin. You will find the camp rules and welcome packet in your bunkhouse. Understand the rules are for your safety. No climbing the water tower, do NOT touch the perimeter fence, and stay away from the waterfall on the far side of the lake. Trespassers will be sent home in a box, if there is anything left after the bears finish with you." With that, Ms. Markum instructed them to finish their dinner in a civilized manner and then head to their bunkhouses for a mandatory lights out at 9:00 pm.

Lee couldn't tell if Ms. Markum was serious about the bears, but he wasn't about to test her. He was going to eat. Lee did not need any encouragement. With his mom not there to ration his portions to a maximum of 1800 calories, he heaped his plate full of spaghetti and meatballs, garlic bread, and two pieces of apple pie. He passed on the squishy looking green beans—he didn't need green calories—and grabbed two glasses of juice.

Balancing the heavy tray, Lee scoped out the room looking for a good place to sit. There was still an open seat next to the boy with the leather jacket and the cool sunglasses. Lee walked slowly toward them, watching and listening.

The girl with wild curls leaned across the table from Tex, her hands always moving.

"Why'd you stupid boys have to ruin our first night?" Curls said.

"Who died and made you camp monitor?" Tex was now nose-to-nose with Curls.

"I'm Ria Santos," she said. "And I don't have to take any lip from a muscle-head like you." She grabbed her tray and stormed off, while Tex mimicked her wild movements.

Lee reversed direction, hunkering down at an almost empty table. He focused on the plate in front of him. The noises in his stomach died down as mouthfuls of noodles, sauce and meatballs hit the spot. The food was great. According to the weekly menu, tomorrow would be German night. If the labs are as good as advertised, maybe he could find a way to fit in and the summer wouldn't be a complete loss.

Lee scanned the room for the possibility of seconds. The food line had closed, but cafeteria workers were circulating around the tables. Maybe he could still snag a little something extra. The workers moved in pairs and wore latex gloves. One carried a roster of names, checking each camper's nametag against the list. Lee watched with growing curiosity when the worker carefully took each camper's drink glass as they got up to leave. The first worker handed the dirty glass to the second, mouthing the number from the roster. The second worker dumped the contents of each glass into a plastic bin before slipping the glass into a bag marked with the corresponding number. The bag looked like the sterile ones he used in his lab at home.

Hellooo Einstein! No one else seemed to notice this strange collection of glassware. Should he say something? No, he'd be branded a paranoid weirdo on his very first day. Lee decided to test a hypothesis instead by grabbing his glass with his napkin and sliding it under the table. There he wiped it clean inside and out with a discarded napkin, before placing it back on the table in front of him.

That's when Lee saw the leather bomber jacket on the move. Tex, and a boy who made Tex look tiny in comparison, grabbed their trays and headed out. Figures Tex would hang out with him. Probably a football or a soccer player, like all the popular guys at school. It was not mathematically probable they would hang around with him. They were two steps away. Now was Lee's chance to join them. But the magnetic force was back, holding him down.

So he dug his fork into a piece of cake rejected by the kid across from him. Only Lee's arm and fork were free to move.

— • — • • • — • • • — — • — — — — — — — • • •

As the campers drifted off to sleep, behind a vaulted door in a windowless lab a man in a white lab jacket finished his report. CONTROL had ordered the utmost attention to the specimens. The man was pleased with his discoveries. However, he knew CONTROL would have a different reaction.

Memo for the Record
Date/Time: 15 JUN/0345Z
To: CONTROL
From: BIOLAB
Re: Operation Mess

DNA samples were successfully collected from all campers by way of biosensors and saliva specimens, with one exception. All samples were verified against security database with two exceptions.

Data sent to security to investigate and eliminate possible infiltrators.

② Shocking Security

Audrey Rochais half-skipped, half-danced along the path through the woods. She had made a stop at the bunkhouse to brush her teeth after breakfast and was running late to the assembly area for the first series of tests. She came to a fork in the path and veered right. The morning sun filtered through the trees keeping the air cool. Audrey did three *chassés* followed by a *petit jeté*, just the way her ballet teacher, Madam Françoise, taught her.

The dance chased away her general sense of dread. A lumpy mattress and a new sleeping bag that smelled like iodine had kept her up most of the night, not to mention nightmares of killer meatballs. The other girls in her cabin, especially Hannah Martin, did their best to make her feel less embarrassed about getting splattered at the food fight. Hannah knew just what to do and say. She had a way of tilting her head and peering at you through thick lashes that gave her an exotic and mysterious air. Audrey hoped after the aptitude tests, they could hang out and maybe become best friends.

Audrey twirled at another split in the path. She didn't remember the trail between the bunkhouse and the mess hall having this many choices. Something crunched in the leafy undergrowth. A tree crackled above her. The back of her neck tingled. There was an odd hum as a hawk soared over her head and disappeared from sight. She could not shake the feeling that something or someone was watching her. She could hear her mom telling her to stop being so oversensitive, but she couldn't. It was her mom that made her that way.

She twisted right among the thick brambles and the steep hillside, only to be sent back the direction she had come from. But this time she noticed a sign mounted on a post: *No Hunting. No Exceptions.* She hadn't remembered seeing it before. She lurched down one path before spinning around. She had reached a fence. How could she be so lost?

The screeching of two squirrels stopped her. A hunk of bread flew through the air, landing in the crook of a branch. One of the squirrels snatched it. Then it leapt from the branch, flying through the air, over the fence to a tree on the other side.

The second squirrel screamed and pranced and shook the branch. A second piece of bread went flying. The squirrel bounded to where it was caught in the leaves. The branch bent before it snapped, sending the squirrel and limb plunging toward the fence. There was a crack. Sparks flew. Audrey covered her eyes. The acrid smell of singed fur filled the air.

"Don't move," said a voice next to her.

Audrey screeched, colliding with an Asian boy with big eyes behind thick-framed glasses.

"Sorry," Lee Wong said. "I didn't mean to startle you. I was worried you'd touch the fence." He pointed to the metal that had fried the squirrel. A faded neon-orange sign read, *HIGH VOLTAGE. KEEP AWAY*. In his hand he held a black box the size of a deck of cards with a wire and metal clip attached to one end. "My voltmeter says the fence is not set to stun." He stuck out his left hand, "I'm Lee, by the way."

"Audrey." She tried to catch her breath and not think about the poor squirrel Tears stung her eyes as she reached for his hand. She wasn't being polite. She needed to get a better sense of him, to know if he was friend or foe. It took a moment before his warm, soft hand folded gently into hers.

"You're the girl that got hammered by spaghetti last night."

"Do you think everyone noticed?"

Lee blushed. His big, black eyes transformed into what looked like upside down smiles. He returned his hand to his pocket.

"I don't think I like this place," Audrey whispered. If she could only find her way out of the woods and into class, she'd feel much better.

"I know what you mean. Weird stuff's been going on."

A sense of relief washed over Audrey. She wasn't the only one who noticed things were off. With all the distractions, she had forgotten why she had even come to this place. It was the nation's premier foreign language and culture camp.

"Oui! Do you speak Chinese?"

"Chinese? Ah, sorry, never learned." Lee looked at Audrey, confused.

"Not a word? I'm fluent in French." She leaned in to sense if he was teasing her.

"Egg Foo Yung?"

Audrey sighed. "I love Chinese food. 4, 8, 12, 25, 30 and 99. I always get the same numbers in my fortune cookies. I think it's a sign."

"Speaking of signs, did you notice the guys with the clipboards last night—"

"Which language classes did you sign up for?" Audrey interrupted. "I'm taking Mandarin Chinese and Farsi." She didn't want to talk about the mess at dinner, or Eric Little the counselor who accused her of trying to steal his wallet. She was only trying to help him up. He probably had her on some list now. "Oh no!" Audrey squealed.

"You think they want our fingerprints?" Lee's eyes were now full moons.

"No. We're late for testing. I'm so turned around, I'll never find my way back."

Lee shoved his hands deeper in his pockets. "I know the way. Follow me?"

Audrey hooked her arm around Lee's. She could feel his shyness. She liked that. It was like an invitation to share secrets.

— • — • • — • • — — • — — — — — — • •

Memo for the Record
Date/Time: 16 JUN/2124Z
To: Security for SPOT
Info: CONTROL
From: BULLDOG
Re: Suspicious Behavior: Camper Rochais

Recommend flagging security file of camper Audrey Rochais. Subject tried to pick my pockets during the food fight, although subject insisted she slipped. This morning I observed her heading toward an off-limits part of the woods. I tracked her to the perimeter fence. She was joined by Lee Wong. The meeting appeared accidental, but given the security alert, may not have been.

③

Good Cowboy, Bad Cowboy

Tex Shaker ran. His body had been itching to move for the last hour. He was done with school—forever! Tall and strong, he was made for the outdoors. His idea of fun was speed, noise and danger. At the age of 11, his name was added to the Guiness World Records book when he became the youngest boy to solo in a glider. Sure, he had to go to Mexico to fly because they didn't have any stupid rules about being over 14 to glide or 16 to fly an airplane. Not that Tex let rules get in his way, but breaking them somehow made the world record even sweeter. At 12, he broke records around the globe in the Maugobi Desert Cross-Country Grand Prix.

He should have been racing this summer, but he had just lost his cousin in a fiery crash, and with that his desire to ever drive again. The subject was too painful for him even to think about. So, he hadn't needed too much prodding from his ma to come to Camp International. At least it was away from home. But after two days, he was going stir-crazy. Camp International was a big mistake.

Tex punched his arms into the air in an act of frustration and release. For a moment he felt free. Suddenly the ground disappeared, and he lost his balance, starting a long, uncontrolled roll down the grassy hill. His body came to an abrupt stop on top of a soft lump.

"Get off me! I can't breathe," the lump protested. Tex laughed, but the lump pushed him up with stunning force. The next moment, Lee flipped and pinned Tex to the ground.

"Nice move, partner. Didn't know you're a wrestling champ." Tex slapped Lee on the shoulder, signaling to be released.

"Luck, I guess." Lee panted as he stood, and stuck out his hand to help Tex. Tex grabbed it, then yanked Lee's arm, flipping him to the ground and pinning him.

"UNCLE," Lee gasped.

"You okay dude?" Tex looked down at Lee's blotchy face. He recognized the asthmatic breathing; his sister had the same problem. Texas ragweed set her off every year and had sent her to the hospital more than a couple of times.

Lee managed to nod as he wheezed.

"Can you believe how they lied about this place?" Tex ripped fistfuls of grass. "We're supposed to be learning survival skills. What a bunch of baloney. It's all boring tests and books."

"I thought this was supposed to be a science camp," Lee said. "Do you know a girl named Audrey? She thinks it's a language camp. What is it?"

"Don't care. I'm breaking outta here first chance I get."

"What makes you think they'll let you?"

"Let me?" Tex squinted his eyes.

"The fence is hot. Audrey and I saw it fry a squirrel this morning. We're pretty much trapped."

"That's odd," Tex said. "They're jamming signals too. I tried to use my cell phone to call home. I have full bars, or at least my phone says so, but when you try to call, something breaks the connection."

"I'm telling you, we're hermetically sealed. I tried to use the pay phone outside of Ms. Markum's office. It doesn't work either. I've been watching the staff. They're doing some really weird stuff. It's not just these crazy tests, it's like we're lab animals the way they watch us. There's no way to escape—"

"Escape to where?" a voice behind them said. It was Marvin Ames.

"Whatcha want?" Tex asked, his eyes narrowing. He stood to face Marvin. "You spying on us?" Tex studied the thin-faced boy with bony knees who shared their bunkhouse. He had started the food fight the first night, which wasn't a big deal, except he tried to pin it on Tex when the counselors started asking questions.

"No." Marvin waved his hand, batting away Tex's accusation. "I thought since we were roomies and everything—"

"Sure, join us," Lee said.

Tex was about to tell Marvin to get lost when Hannah Martin caught his attention. She was standing at the top of the hill watching him. She was tall and thin, all legs like a colt. She gave him a flirty wave with her fingers and smiled before walking away. Tex didn't get it. All of a sudden girls were drawn to him like bees to honey, and he was allergic to bees. It was time to move on.

"Where are you guys from? And how'd you hear about this camp?" Marvin asked as Tex started to leave.

Marvin was acting all twitchy. Tex had a knack for reading people. Maybe it was because he grew up on a ranch, and the ranch hands came in two kinds: good cowboys and bad cowboys. The first kind worked hard and helped out his pa. The bad ones caused trouble. Marvin smelled like a bad one.

"Why'd you come?" Tex scooped up four small stones from the gravel path and aimed for a metal garbage can affixed to a concrete pad twenty feet away. He remembered a trick his pa's favorite ranch hand had taught Tex to clear snakes from the trail. The sound of rocks hitting another rock or tree was enough to scare them away. The stones hit the side of the can within centimeters of each other, making a noticeable dent. Marvin jumped. Snakes didn't stand a chance against Tex.

— • — • • • — • • • — — • — — — — • •

Memo for the Record
Date/Time: 16 JUN/4124Z
To: Security
Info: CONTROL
From: COMMO
Re: Damage Assessment

Jamming transmitter XJ32 (trash can concealment) was extensively damaged this afternoon by a camper and is no longer in working condition. Estimated cost of repair: $63,500. Estimated time of repair: one week, if parts are available.

From video coverage, it appears equipment was damaged on purpose. While it is unlikely those responsible knew the nature of the sensitive equipment, recommend Security and Administration take corrective action against the troublemakers: Lee Wong, Tex Shaker and Marvin Ames.

④
Falling into a Spy Trap

It had been a week of bizarre tests, and none of them had anything to do with chemistry, biology or physics, as far as Lee could tell. The counselors only laughed when he asked if he was at the wrong camp. Lee shuffled in line, nervous. It wasn't just the tests. His secret stash of snacks was dwindling, and according to his calculations, they would not last the 53 days left of camp. He had already tried to find a way to sneak past the camera trained on the mess hall entrance, with no success. He planned to try again after Eric Little finished team assignments.

Teams for what? The unknown worried Lee. So did Eric. Audrey was convinced Eric was not what he seemed, but Lee couldn't follow Audrey's disjointed logic to understand exactly what bothered her.

"Hey, Wong." Eric motioned to Lee to stand with the Alpha team. Tex, Audrey and Jennifer Bragg, a girl he didn't know, had already been picked for Alpha. He was happy to be with Tex (Mr. Cool) and Audrey, even if she was a little peculiar.

"Alpha and Kappa teams follow me. Everyone else, your leaders will be here shortly. Wait for them." Eric set a wicked pace into the woods.

Kappa team pushed their way in behind Eric with Marvin in the lead.

Tex nudged Lee. "Glad we're not stuck with him."

Lee agreed. There was something piranha-like about him that kept Lee from getting too close.

"He's my second LFP in this dumb camp."

Tex didn't say who his number one least favorite person was, but Lee had been watching and had a theory. He'd bet his new set of beakers it was another member of Kappa: Ria Santos. Every time Tex and Ria came within five feet of each other, it was like watching a chemical reaction, the flash of dry ice coming in contact with fiery magnesium.

"Too bad there aren't any real bears around here. I'd like to see Marvin cut the food line with one of those bad boys."

"What makes you think the instructors lied about the bears?" Lee lowered his voice.

"Grownups are always trying to scare us so we can't have fun. If I followed the rules, I wouldn't be driving, let alone racing."

Tex was driving already? Lee sighed. The counselors definitely made a mistake. He should be on Kappa team with the other social rejects. He could trade with either Penbrook Westerhouse or Hannah Martin, who deserved to be on a cooler team. Lee had talked to Hannah once. She made him nervous the way she stared at him through a screen of dark eyelashes. Audrey said Hannah was so sweet and helpful. Penbrook was the kind who wouldn't even notice if Lee was alive. He wore expensive polo shirts—today a red one with a blue alligator logo. Penbrook looked down his nose at the not-so-cool kids.

"Let's move it, ladies." Eric was relentless.

"Oh, Einstein, save me," Lee muttered under his breath. "Not another one of these survivor games. Pleeeese let a science lab be our destination and not some obstacle course." For the past six days, he had been subjected to the strangest tests. Like the one that gave him less than an hour to answer 100 questions on his likes and dislikes. Would he rather be a fireman or a dress designer? He didn't want to be either, but there was no option for "none of the above." By the time the test was over, he had no idea what he liked or disliked, other than the test.

Then there was the dark booth where images flashed on a screen for seconds. He was expected to describe the images in detail. Sure, he could remember the big stuff, like there was a room, with a sofa, two chairs, five bookshelves and three paintings. But he couldn't remember how many books were on the shelf, or the color of the carpet. Yes, a man was sitting in one of the chairs reading a magazine. No, he didn't notice the title, or the kind of shoes the man was wearing. No amount of begging by the campers would get the instructor to show the images a second time.

After 15 minutes of strenuous motion, Lee's face burned hot. He stumbled and wheezed, kicking up clouds of dust. Audrey coughed behind him. Did she notice the sweat dribbling down his back? After today, she'd probably decide she'd rather hang out with Tex. His glasses were completely fogged. As he reached to clear his lenses, a hand gripped his shoulder.

"We're here girls." From a battered messenger bag, Eric pulled out two small rolls of paper secured by rubber bands. He handed one to Lee and one to Ria.

"You have 30 minutes to find the locations on your maps. This is a team exercise." Eric smiled. It wasn't a nice, warm smile. He looked like a cat that had swallowed a mouse. "Oh, by the way, avoid tipping off the other teams on what you're doing, because the last team to finish gets latrine duty. Oops, now there's only 28 minutes."

Lee watched Eric disappear down the trail. Maybe Audrey was right about him. During one of their tests, the room had become unbearably hot, like someone had turned the heater on high. When Lee asked if he could open a window, Eric told him to keep his eyes focused on the test in front of him. Then Eric poured a glass of water from a pitcher, stirring the ice in his glass so the cubes clinked each time he took a sip.

"Okay outdoor babies," Tex said after Eric was out of earshot. "I'll take the map so we don't get lost. Or eaten by bears." Tex winked at Lee.

Lee stumbled hard over a tree root, his chest tightening as he fell. He would be the first choice for any carnivore. Soft and chewy. Plenty to gnaw on.

Hannah from Kappa helped Lee to his feet and offered him a damp towelette. Audrey was right; she was helpful.

"Eric gave the maps to Lee and me." Ria's long springy curls bounced around her head, making her look twice as tall as she actually was. She looked directly at Tex. "We call the shots."

Unlike some of the other kids, Ria talked to him. A lot. Her family was originally from Venezuela, and she spoke Spanish fluently. While Audrey was impressed by this, Lee had concluded Ria was the smartest girl in camp. She hadn't missed a single question on any of the tests, and she made sure everyone knew it.

Lee looked at Tex.

"Right?" Ria said a little louder.

"Ahhhh…." What could he say that wouldn't have Tex wondering whose side he was on, or make Ria hopping mad. Ria had a fierce temper.

"We're Alpha. You're Kappa." Tex snatched the paper from Lee. "Different maps." He waved it in front of her for extra emphasis.

"I bet he's watching," Audrey whispered. "Have you noticed the counselors seem to know where we are and what we're up too?" She looked over her shoulder then at the sky before adding, "It gives me the creeps."

"You losers can hold hands and bond if you want. I have more important things to do," sneered Penbrook from Kappa team before he turned into the woods. Lee could hear the echo of a stick hitting trees long after Penbrook disappeared.

"This exercise is stupid. I'm going back to camp," said Jennifer, the fourth member of Alpha team. She added an extra layer of lip-gloss before heading in the opposite direction of Penbrook. Lee secretly wished Audrey would decide to follow Jennifer so he would have an excuse to head back to camp, too. He was certain their map wasn't leading to anything good.

"Wait!" Audrey called after Jennifer. "We're supposed to work together. You know, like a team?" Jennifer's bright pink shirt disappeared into a sea of green.

"What do we do now?" Audrey's voice jumped an octave between 'what' and 'now'.

"We follow our map," Ria said. Lee heard her mutter something under her breath about being stuck with losers.

"Maybe since Jennifer left, I could join Alpha team?" Marvin said to Tex and Lee.

"Maybe you're already on a team." Ria grabbed Marvin's shirt and pulled him back. She glared at Tex. "Have fun cleaning toilets."

"Have fun cleaning toilets," Tex aped as Ria, Hannah and Marvin started down the trail. Ria stopped and turned back. Lee groaned. Ria's black eyes were sparking. Tex had to do it, prime the chemical explosion. They'd never finish, let alone start, this exercise if he didn't stop Tex. Maybe part of the test was how they acted under pressure, like when he watched his mice navigate a maze. Whatever skills the instructors were looking for, he was pretty sure it wasn't on how well they could bicker.

Audrey got to Tex first, grabbing his hand and pulling him in the opposite direction. Tex growled but focused on the map he had snatched from Lee. "Our map has a center point with five spokes. Our target is 2500 feet down one of the spokes. See these?" Tex pointed to curved lines on the map. "Elevation markers. We need to climb. We have five choices. I say we split up and find which ones head up hill."

"Splitting up is completely illogical; it's a team exercise. We have to finish together," Lee said, feet not moving an inch. If they were being watched, he wanted them to know he made decisions based on logic. Plus, he didn't want to be left alone with the bears.

"My lucky number is five." Audrey flashed Lee a smile. "So that's the way we should go."

"How do you figure that?" Tex muttered.

"It's a feeling. Sometimes I just know. It's like when you feel like you've been somewhere before, even though you haven't."

"Yeah," Tex said, although he still looked confused.

Lee said nothing, deciding to keep his thoughts to himself. The sooner they chose a path, the sooner they'd be done, right or wrong, and he'd have a rest and a snack and then he would try to figure out how Audrey's brain worked.

The route Audrey chose hugged the lake for 500 feet before heading straight up. It looked to Lee like a mountain goat created it, and Audrey was part goat by the way she bounded ahead.

"What are we looking for?" she called back.

"No idea." Lee gasped between words. He could feel the wheezing in his chest.

Tex held up the map. "The contour lines mark a depression at the top. It's oblong. In the center, there is an X."

"Great, another one of those 'X marks the spot' kind of clues," Lee grumbled.

Lee was hot, sweaty, tired of the steady climb and certain they were going to fail.

"Wait. I hear something," Audrey whispered.

"My stomach?" Lee clutched his belly.

"No, voices."

"Hide!" Tex said.

They dove behind thick brush on the side of the trail, moments before another team rushed by. Flat on his back among a patch of thistles, Lee watched a hawk gliding low in a slow pass over their heads before flying up above the treetops and disappearing from sight.

"I know you're both going to think I'm crazy, but I swear that bird is following us," Audrey said, her eyes also on the sky.

Lee wanted to tell her that in the food chain humans hunt birds, not the other way around, but his throat was closing, and he couldn't breathe. He fumbled with the pocket on the side of his cargo shorts, fingering through the many odds and ends he carried just in case.

Tex rolled next to him, freeing the inhaler jammed in Lee's pocket. Lee managed to sit up, the wheezing in his chest slowing.

"You okay?" Tex said.

"Ye…a…h." Lee used the break to take off his shoe and poke at a blister on his heel.

"Ten minutes before we blow this assignment. Any ideas?" Tex said.

"Lee can find his way out of any place," Audrey said.

"Only once I've been there. I have a photographic memory." Lee struggled with his shoe.

"That way." Audrey turned toward a thick stand of trees. She had a look in her eyes as if an unseen force had whispered the answer in her ear. Despite his better judgment, Lee followed Audrey and Tex followed Lee. She led them through the trees into a small clearing, shaped like an oval. In the center stood a weathered post. A *No Hunting* sign bolted to it was similar to the ones Lee had seen around the perimeter of the camp. Tex kicked the tall grass with his boot, searching the ground for anything that looked like it had been left for them. Lee dropped to his knees and examined the sign.

No Hunting. No EXception.

This sign was different from all the others. The *X* was in capital letters, and it looked like the print was slightly raised. He ran his fingers over it before pushing on the center of the *X*.

The ground gave way. Lee hit bottom, not with a thud, but a bounce. He heard Audrey scream. Tex and Audrey landed next to him and bounced into the air again, before becoming tangled in a pile of arms and legs.

"You made it just in time." Ms. Markum checked her stopwatch as the trampoline absorbed the energy from their fall. "Welcome to Junior Spy Camp."

— • — • • • — • • • — — • — — — — • •

Memo for the Record
Date/Time: 22 JUN/1524Z
To: CONTROL
Info: SPOT
From: TRAIL
Re: IMINT from Operation Map – Alpha and Kappa teams

Security officers SPOT and TRAIL monitored Alpha and Kappa teams via the low-altitude hawk drone, obtaining live imagery during the exercise. The teams demonstrated indecision at the beginning, with two recruits breaking off (STAR-SHOOTER and IVY-BONES).

The remaining recruits split into designated teams. Kappa team was the first to locate target access point. PUZZLE-GIRL assumed the lead, routinely consulting NIGHT-WIND, but not EAGLE-EYES.

Alpha team's movements suggested disagreement among the recruits. No clear leader was evident from imagery. Alpha was the last team to locate target access point.

STAR-SHOOTER and IVY-BONES failed to complete the assignment. STAR-SHOOTER did not appear to try, backtracking at a brisk pace on the trail to the bunkhouses. She stopped twice, appearing concerned about her hair and makeup.

IVY-BONES left the path and unwisely cut through the poison ivy to cross the mud bog. He required exfiltration after getting stuck in mud up to his hips. Security delivered him to the Medical unit.

NOTE: IVY-BONES has an attitude. Security let him wallow in the mud for an hour to learn some respect for nature.

⑤

The Recruitment

"WAHOOO!" Tex hollered, untangling himself from Audrey. "Did you say spy camp?"

Ms. Markum didn't respond, but signaled for them to follow her. As Tex's eyes adjusted to the dim light, he could just make out the contours of an underground tunnel. Cool air filled the space, carrying with it an odd odor. Spy camp? Was she playing a joke on them?

She stopped in front of a metal door set into a wall. The door had no handle or any obvious way to be opened. She turned her head in profile and held still. Tex looked at Lee who pointed up, mouthing "camera." Tex looked a second before they heard a click. The door swung inward. He didn't see any sign of a hidden camera.

Tex ran his hands around the inside edges where the lock should be. Where was the mechanism? He let Lee and Audrey pass so he could examine the door. He rapped on the edge of it with his fist, but the door closed in on him. He jumped clear, entering a room even darker than the first, and plowed into Audrey.

She let out a high pitch whine. "I don't...I feel...get me out." Audrey's fingers dug into his forearm. Her face glowed white in the dim light.

"Stick with me, Aud, you'll be okay." Tex's bravado hid the growing knot in the pit of his stomach. He had no idea how they got in, let alone how they'd get out. She could stick to him, but he was sticking to Ms. Markum.

As Ms. Markum stepped across the room, a row of small lights recessed in the floor marked a path, which ended near the far wall. There the lights formed a soccer goal-sized rectangle on the floor around a narrow marble column.

Tex edged forward to get a better view. "Pardon me, Ma'am." Tex hopped back after stepping on Ms. Markum's foot.

Ms. Markum winked at Tex and without even looking back said, "Lee, please try to keep up with the rest of us."

Sure enough, Lee was lingering by the metal door. Tex had never met a kid like Lee before. That boy moved so slow, dead flies wouldn't fall off him. Everything was slow about him, except for his eyes and his brain. He missed nothing and figured things out twice as fast as Tex. Like how the entire camp was really an electric cage. If it weren't for Lee's warning about the fence, Tex would have been fried just like the squirrel. That would have seriously messed with his escape plan. And if he'd given the camp the slip, he would not be standing in this underground room following a trail of light to a dream come true.

"Thanks, dude." Tex slapped Lee on the back when he came alongside him.

"For what?"

Tex grinned. He needed to focus on Ms. Markum. She pulled a badge from one of her many pockets on her vest and placed it on an optical reader mounted in the center of the column. "CONTROL. M-Y-8-6-2," she said with the precision of a computer-generated voice. "Down."

The floor dropped and a high-density Plexiglas wall slid up to enclose them.

"Eeeeee!" Audrey screamed. She grabbed at the air searching for something to cling to.

Tex's ears hurt. He grabbed Audrey by the shoulders and held her. The screaming stopped, and her shoulders relaxed. That's when he let go; fast. He had touched a girl on purpose. What was he thinking?

Ms. Markum ignored all of it. Her command stopped the elevator at Level 3-A. This was a clear glass room;

empty except for what looked like a shower stall in one corner. Ms. Markum stepped in and turned a nozzle. Poof. She disappeared momentarily into a cloud of steam.

"One at a time," she motioned.

Tex stepped in first. As the fine mist hit him, he waved his arms above his head and sank toward the floor, crying out in a falsetto "I'm melting."

"Keep it moving," Ms. Markum said. Her voice was like a block of ice, trying to freeze all things funny.

"That's got to be hard on the hair." Audrey smoothed back her ponytail before stepping into the stall.

When it was Lee's turn, he crouched down and examined the floor.

"There's a sensor. Is it a decontamination device?"

Ms. Markum wasn't giving any explanations. She moved to a second glass door, opposite the elevator. Tex stayed glued to her heels, not wanting to miss a thing. The door slid open. They entered a corridor, no longer high-tech and glossy, but with painted walls like the inside of a house—an ugly house where the owner favored drab green and dirty gray. It looked normal except for the doors lining the corridor. Dial combination locks replaced doorknobs. What secrets did they hide? Lee tested one. It didn't budge.

"Do you think we'll learn to pick locks?" Tex whispered to Lee.

"Is this place for real?" Lee asked. He touched the door

like he expected it not to be solid. Lee's face was flushed with excitement, and his eyes were wide, like a camera lens.

On the floor were two painted lines. The blue line led to their right. The red line went to the left. Ms. Markum followed the blue line, which zigged and zagged along a series of corridors, up a flight of stairs and along two more corridors. Here the doors had windows. Tex peered into the first one and saw an oval table in the center of the room and workstations around the perimeter.

"Is this where we'll get our mission assignments?" Tex said.

"Thank you Einstein." Lee pressed his face to the glass of the door opposite Tex. "I'm never going back."

Inside, Tex saw a lab with Petri dishes, microscopes, Bunsen burners and beakers. "So they weren't lying about those labs." They moved to the next window. This room was filled with the latest woodworking equipment.

"Oh, look!" Audrey pointed into another room. "A photography studio."

Tex had a pretty good built-in sense of direction, but all the twisting and turning disoriented even him. They were still underground, but exactly where in relationship to the tunnel they fell through, he didn't have a clue.

Ms. Markum stopped in front of two sets of large double doors. Like all the doors they had passed, the one in front of him was identified only by a number/letter combination: 3C25. It opened into a well-lit auditorium.

Excited chatter filled the air. Tex stood in the doorway. It looked like there were about 35 campers in the room, all of whom he recognized.

Audrey and Lee squeezed into the doorway.

"There's that creep Marvin." Tex struck his head with his hand thinking he must not be seeing straight if that dead-ender was in the room.

"He's not the only one from Kappa team." Audrey pointed across the room. "I see Ria and Hannah here too."

Tex groaned. Sure enough, there was Ria, bouncing up and down, while talking to Hannah Martin, the only member of Kappa who wasn't completely annoying. Marvin caught sight of Tex and motioned to them to sit in his row. Tex looked away and resumed scanning the room. All of Kappa team was in the auditorium, except for Penbrook.

Brenton Meyer, Connor Philips and J.J. Dean of Omega team were there too. Tex shared the bunkhouse with the three of them, and they had had several arm-wrestling contests the last few nights. Brenton was unbeatable. They were a cool team, unlike Kappa.

Tex recognized kids from Zeta, Epsilon, Iota and Theta. A lot of teams were not there, like Delta. Mr. Corwin said their performance during the tests would determine their opportunities. So the past week was a try-out for becoming spies? And Delta didn't make the cut?

Audrey grabbed Tex and pulled him away from the door. She headed toward the back of the auditorium. She looked pale again. Why was she so freaked? Didn't she understand they'd been especially picked out for spy camp?

Ms. Markum stepped onto the stage, and the room grew still, except for Lee's stomach. Tex could hear it growling so clearly he thought it was his.

"Welcome Junior Spy recruits." Ms. Markum paused as murmurs ran around the room. Her voice was warmer, but still remained firm. "The first order of business is the packet on your seats. Take out the Secrecy Agreement. Read it and sign it. If you do not agree with the terms, please raise your hand, and you will be escorted out."

Tex ripped into the manila envelope and removed an official looking form titled "Camp Rules."

"Ouch!" Audrey had her finger in her mouth. There was a smear of bright red next to the red SECRET stamped at the top of the page.

Tex laughed. "I don't think you have to sign your name in blood for this to be official." He scribbled his signature without reading any further.

"Does anyone have a band aid?" Audrey whispered, wiping the page clean while trying to stop the bleeding. The papers spilled to the floor. Tex shook his head as he collected them. Audrey didn't fit his idea of a spy.

"I can make one." Lee pulled an empty M&M wrapper out of his pocket. He wrapped it around her finger, fastening it with blob of epoxy glue.

"What else you got in there?" Tex cocked his head to see inside the cargo pocket.

"Stuff I picked up off the trail. Kids will throw anything away. This is good glue."

Ms. Markum droned on about secrecy. Tex could care less about the rules. He was going to be a spy.

He figured Audrey cared since she was reading parts of the text out loud.

"This Agreement binds the undersigned to protect the classified information learned through his or her association with the Junior Spy Program, under the penalty of law. Should any recruit knowingly disclose secret information, the recruit could be tried under the Espionage Act and be subjected to life in a maximum-security prison in solitary confinement—"

"What does *binding into perpetuity* mean?" Audrey asked.

"You can't talk about the program even after you die, I guess," Lee said. "If you think that's extreme, look at this. *Solitary confinement.* That's like being grounded for life, with no phone, TV or anything. They must be serious about this secrecy stuff."

"You signing?" Audrey whispered.

"You bet. Did you see those labs?" Lee asked.

Tex watched Audrey. Her eyes were closed as she twisted her necklace, like she might strangle herself. What was her problem? Back in the woods, Audrey said she felt like they were being watched. Did she feel better now they knew the truth? Or did Audrey know something Tex didn't?

Eric Little had reached their row. Tex and Lee handed over their papers at the same time. Tex reached over for Audrey's as she scribbled her name with her left hand. He noticed the bandaged finger of her right hand tucked behind her back, fingers crossed.

— • — • • • — • • • — — • — — — — • •

Memo for the Record
Date/Time: 22 JUN/1524Z
To: CONTROL
From: SPOT, Security
Re: Operation Bait and Switch

Five recruits declined to sign the Secrecy Agreement: Joy Berkmann (Omega), Tomas Sanchez (Zeta), Leo Parnetti (Epsilon), Gina Whitehall (Zeta) and Olga Chilova (Iota).

Per standard procedure, these recruits have been selected out of the Program and returned to Camp International's medical center for treatment of sun exposure and hallucinations. They will be monitored for a few days before being sent home. Teams Zeta, Epsilon, Iota and Omega have been given briefings to help them answer questions their former teammates might pose while remaining at camp.

Additionally, two campers were eliminated for non-suitability from the recruit list prior to being exposed to the secret facilities: STAR-SHOOTER (Alpha) and IVY BONES (Kappa). They have been placed into new camp teams and will be monitored for inappropriate interest in the activities of their former team members.

6

Switching to Spy Identities

Lee settled into a chair that swiveled at the large oval table of Classroom 3D01, the home base for Alpha team for the duration of their training. Everything was happening too fast. He wasn't sure what was real and what was not. Falling into spy camp seemed no more real than disappearing into a black hole in outer space. However, the pledge of secrecy he had signed an hour and fifteen minutes ago did. Too real. He hoped the lab was real, too.

Four white binders with SECRET stamped on their spines were positioned in front of the four chairs. Mr. Corwin sat in the fifth with a coffee cup and no binder. Lee glanced at Audrey and Tex. Audrey sat with her eyes closed and looked like she might be sick. Where was Jennifer? He hadn't seen her in the auditorium either. Four small desks with computer and photography equipment lined two walls. Each desk had a two-drawer safe, complete with combination lock. A larger desk was in the front corner of the room. Next to it was a safe and a large paper trash bag. A wide whiteboard hung on the wall. There was no clutter, loose papers or personal items in the room.

"Call me MOLECHECK." Mr. Corwin swiveled in his chair at the head of the table, a mischievous glint in his eye. Lee had noticed Mr. Corwin's tie earlier, but up close, he could see that what he mistook for little stickmen were really the white scientific drawings of the molecules that made up caffeine. Science geek humor. Lee didn't dare laugh.

"Going forward, we will use codenames only."

Tex let loose a catcall. It figures, Lee thought. Tex was made for spy school. He probably already knew everything about spying. Tex had no fear. Lee tried to imagine himself a spy—the shootouts, high-speed car chases, hang gliding into secret military installations—him alone against the bad guys. Not.

"Ms. Markum, who you will now refer to as CONTROL, gave you a lot of information this morning. Do you have any questions?"

Lee had about one hundred spinning in his brain like positive ions in search of missing electrons. Before he could decide which one to ask, Audrey raised her hand.

"Mr. Corwin, what happened to the kids who didn't sign the secrecy papers?"

"MOLECHECK. Codenames only. Those who did not sign have been removed."

"Removed to where?" Audrey asked.

MOLECHECK took off his glasses and wiped them with the bottom of his tie. "All you need to know is they will not pose a security threat. Camp International operates as a normal summer camp. You will be trained as spies under the cover of the camp. The regular campers will not be aware of your special activities. It will be your job to blend in and protect the secrecy of the spy school."

Lee studied MOLECHECK. How could he be in two camps at once? He was having a hard enough time keeping up on camp hikes. Now he had to spy, too?

"So we'll become spies?" Tex spun in his chair. "Totally cool."

"Maybe. Maybe not. It depends on you."

Tex stopped in mid-rotation. "What do you mean?"

"You must be certified as a Junior Spy first. For the next seven weeks you will undergo tradecraft training. You'll learn how to recruit agents, write intelligence reports, conduct surveillance, use secret communication techniques, and more. I'm warning you, it's a difficult course. Most of you will be eliminated."

"Elimina—" Audrey twisted her necklace tight.

"Eliminated as in terminated," MOLECHECK said.

"Terminated how?" Audrey's voice reaching a painful octave.

"Concentrate on the training materials and don't break the rules."

"How hard can training be?" Tex asked, raising his arms and locking his fingers behind his neck. He leaned back in his chair, grinning at MOLECHECK.

Lee admired Tex's confidence. He was right. How hard could it be? He had made it this far. Lee copied Tex and eased back in his chair.

"We started with 35 recruits. Five have already been selected out. CONTROL was very clear about the rules and performance standards. If you break them, you're out. There are no second chances."

MOLECHECK's face grew stern, or as stern as it could, with his bushy red eyebrows and dancing eyes. Lee felt MOLECHECK was talking to him and him alone. He slumped low in the chair, almost teetering over. He wondered how long it would be before Ms. Markum realized she'd made a mistake. He should have been cut along with Jennifer. He had more in common with Jennifer than Tex.

"Why all the cloak and dagger?" Tex asked.

"Secrecy is rule number one, two and three in the world of espionage. The Junior Spy Program is nearing its 40th year and is a closely guarded secret of American intelligence," MOLECHECK said. "Not everyone would understand or believe teens could or should be spies. The program might be shut down. That would be a national security tragedy in our view."

MOLECHECK stood and started to pace. "During our years of operation, Junior Spies have been posted in boarding schools across Europe, posed as the children of diplomats, explorers and businessmen, all while secretly running missions. Young people tend to arouse less suspicion than adults. Do not be deceived. Our Junior Spies do not play at being spies. They steal secrets kept by adults, leaders and adversaries around the globe. You may volunteer for missions until you reach the age of 18, or until your cover has been compromised. It is how we protect the program and you."

"What happens when we turn 18?" Audrey asked.

"You retire from spying," MOLECHECK said.

"NO WAY," Tex said.

Lee found his voice. "Why did you pick me?"

MOLECHECK's eyes twinkled. "We need recruits with scientific skills too. I remember one sharp recruit we had here, almost 15 years ago. Brilliant code writer. It was around the time of Y2K—"

"Why to what?" Tex interrupted.

"Y2K, Year Two Thousand, the millennial turnover from 1999 to 2000. Computer clocks weren't designed to change to 2000. We faced a worldwide computer crash."

"I don't remember that," Tex said.

"Precisely. Because it didn't happen. Thanks to the Junior Spy program. Many countries didn't believe we were on the brink of a crisis. Our Junior Spy wrote a computer virus and infected computers running critical infrastructure from Albania to Zimbabwe which secretly fixed the clock problem, keeping air traffic control systems, electricity grids and the like all working on the stroke of midnight, 2000. A lot of people including Americans would have died if not for him."

Lee was stunned. He was being offered a chance of a lifetime to help his country doing something he loved. He could leave all the physical stuff to guys like Tex. Science was his spy weapon.

MOLECHECK straightened his molecular-themed tie. "You all have your strengths, and we will continue to sharpen them while you're here. We'll teach you tradecraft, like disguise, surveillance and secret communication techniques. But I cannot teach you to think, to trust your instincts or to love adventure and intrigue. This summer will quickly determine if you have what it takes."

"Great, let's get started." Tex rocked his chair like he was preparing to catapult out of it.

"Not so fast Tex," MOLECHECK said. "Honesty, loyalty, integrity and courage are the inner traits of a good spy. They also cannot be taught; you either have them or you don't. Most importantly, you cannot be afraid to speak the truth to power."

"Integrity?" Audrey asked.

That surprised Lee, who thought courage would be the hard part.

"Spies often face difficult personal choices, or ethical dilemmas. A good spy does not lose sight of right and wrong. Sometimes the ends can justify the means, but not always. You must stick to your ethics no matter how difficult or painful the results."

"So you decided we'd be good spies from those tests you gave us?" Lee felt a pang in his stomach as he pondered the words "difficult or painful results."

"We've been watching you for a while."

"I knew it," Tex pumped his fist.

"The binder in front of you is your field manual," MOLECHECK said, returning to the ops table. "These manuals will never, repeat never, leave this room. All records of your work and research will be kept in them. For security purposes, the paper will disintegrate if placed in water. Or you can eat it in case of emergency."

Everyone looked at Lee. He opened his manual and sniffed. "What flavor is it?"

MOLECHECK laughed. Soon Audrey and Tex were laughing too. His new friends thought he was funny. The tightness in his stomach eased.

"You will produce a lot a paper writing reports. It must be secured in safes if you plan on keeping it. Paper you don't want does not get thrown in the trash, but in a burn bag." MOLECHECK held up a brown paper bag the size of a large grocery sack. Printed on the side in large print was "Burn".

"So later you put them on a bonfire for the campers to toast their marshmallows?" Tex asked with a laugh.

"Security is no laughing matter," MOLECHECK said. "We burn the bags every couple of days in an incinerator which reduces the secrets to ash." MOLECHECK stood and walked to a two-drawer safe next to the large desk. He pulled out several legal sized envelopes. Flipping through them, he put one back before returning to the oval ops table. He dropped one envelope in front of each of them. "Your codenames."

Tex ripped his envelope across the top and dumped the entire contents on the table while Lee removed each item one by one. Inside Lee found a hard plastic badge with a photo of him taken in the mess hall and a small metallic square embedded next to it. On a separate piece of paper was his codename. Lee was examining the metallic square when Tex stuck his hand out and said,

"Howdy, I'm COW-BOY."

"LAB-MAN," Lee said taking Tex's hand, only to have Tex crush it in his enthusiastic handshake. "That's what the kids at school call me. Or sometimes Lab Rat." Lee immediately wished he hadn't said the last part. He should know better than to let everyone know where he landed on the evolutionary chain.

"I'm MIND-READER, but you know I can't really read minds." Audrey smiled at Lee. "LAB-MAN fits you perfectly." Whatever was bothering her before had passed. Her smile made Lee feel more confident. He was glad they were on the same team.

"Your badge gives you access to the training center and the classified computer system," MOLECHECK explained. "The badge contains a—"

"A biochip," Lee said before he even realized he was talking.

"Yes." MOLECHECK nodded toward Lee. "A microchip with biometric information specific to each of you. Computerized access control will conduct a voice and odor scan of each you and check it against the data stored on the microchip."

"Odor scan? So that explains the puff of steam." Lee's thoughts jumped to the first night at the mess hall, when the cafeteria worker took his glass. "What other biometric samples are stored on this chip?"

"While it's possible to defeat the voice scan," MOLECHECK said, ignoring Lee's question, "the odor sensor is much more difficult to fool."

"We all stink different," Tex said.

"And some more than others," Audrey said with a sniff in Lee's direction, making them all laugh.

"Before we get started, CONTROL asked that I make an announcement. The individual or individuals responsible for glue on the canoe seats are on notice that pranks will not be tolerated at this camp. More than a few Delta team gym shorts were left behind, bonded to the seats. We had several exposed and unhappy campers."

Tex snorted.

"CONTROL was not amused." MOLECHECK's lips curled as he tried to stifle a grin. Lee was the only one not laughing. His fingers wrapped around the tube of glue deep in his cargo pocket. He eyed the burn bag. He needed to lose the glue.

— • — • • • — • • • — — — • — — — — — • •

Memo for the Record
Date/Time: 22 JUN/1630Z
To: CONTROL
From: TRAIL
Re: Counterintelligence Investigation

Security has confirmed Lee Wong's DNA sample with
the one on file. We continue to investigate how the
original sample was contaminated. We have been unable
to eliminate the possibility that it was deliberate and
therefore recommend opening a counterintelligence
investigation of Wong.

Request permission to search Wong's possessions.

Operation Ivanistan

The homeroom went dark. A large map filled the whiteboard. Tex leaned back in his chair, resting his feet on the ops table. Body relaxed, mind sharp, he was ready for his first spy lesson. Fingering his new Junior Spy badge, he watched MOLECHECK with his clownish red hair and weird stick-man tie fumble for what seemed like forever with a laser pointer. The red dot zeroed in on Audrey's forehead, then zipped across the room, landing on the center of the map.

MOLECHECK cleared his throat. "We begin with Operation Ivanistan."

Tex liked the way it sounded: I-VAN-I-STAN. Dangerous. Foreign. A place where he could test his skills and be the best Junior Spy ever.

"This is an imaginary country in which you will learn to be spies. You will complete all your exercises inside this virtual country, and it will come to feel real to you in the next seven weeks. You must live and breathe your cover. Anytime you are outside this room, working in the spy school training environment—not in Camp—the people and situations you encounter will require you to stay in character. You will be tested by situations none of you will be able to predict."

Images flashed on the screen while MOLECHECK explained they would be role-playing. To make it as real as possible, they needed to memorize the smallest details of their identities and Ivanistan.

"Ivanistan is a small country, but its location on the Gulf of Azmaric makes it more important than its size would indicate. The current government is allied with the U.S. At the request of the U.S., it has maintained a strict policy of neutrality on the war between its two neighbors, Michaldom and Samvia..."

Slide blurred into slide. When would he get done talking so they could get to the good stuff? Tex was ready to meet real spies. Would he get his own lock-picking tools? And a ninja outfit with a built-in rappelling cord?

Would they have explosives training? Tex stared at the clock.

"You are American spies in Ivanistan. You must live and breathe your cover…"

MOLECHECK must have said it at least 10 times. Tex's eyes glazed over as data continued to scroll by with information about Ivanistan's employment, government, structure, main imports and exports. Tex glanced at the clock again. He could swear the minute hand did not move. He couldn't sit through much more of this classroom stuff.

MOLECHECK droned on while drawing a big circle on the blackboard with *RECRUITMENT CYCLE* written in the middle. At the top of the circle he wrote *SPOT AND ASSESS*. Tex stared out the narrow window of the door, which had a view of the hallway. Marvin Ames peered in and waved at Tex. How'd that little weasel get out of class? He pressed something against the glass and wiggled it for emphasis. Tex glanced at Audrey, but her back was to the door. Lee must have noticed.

Tex took a white index card from the pile on the table and wrote *Weasel's loose*.

He slipped it to Lee under the table.

Tex frowned when Lee pocketed the note. He jerked his head toward the window several times just as MOLECHECK looked back. Three long strides and a quick twist of the blinds ended the show.

"On this next assignment you will work with a partner." MOLECHECK returned to the front of the room. "MIND-READER will work with LAB-MAN." MOLECHECK pointed to Audrey and Lee. "And, if you haven't noticed by now, Jennifer Bragg did not make the first cut. She will be spending the rest of camp studying exciting topics like Norwegian ice carving. So COW-BOY, you'll partner with PUZZLE-GIRL from Kappa for this one. Teams will shift as you progress through training so we can observe how well you work with different personalities."

Tex bolted upright. Teams? He was the lone ranger; he didn't need a partner, especially a girl.

"You'll work together to learn your aliases and practice your cover story. Do not confuse aliases with your codenames. Aliases are used for operations and will change from mission to mission. We use codenames in-house, in the homeroom for training, in your personnel files and forever more, to protect your identity. Clear?"

Audrey raised her hand an inch above her head. "So I don't get to be me anymore?"

"You do not give up your life, or your family and friends. While in spy school, training, working, writing reports, we'll use codenames. In the camp, you are Audrey. At the end of the summer, if you make it that long, you'll go home as Audrey. If Tex is certified and he contacts you about a mission, he'll identify himself as COW-BOY."

"You mean when," Tex cut in impatiently. "We get it. What's our mission? Can we start now?"

MOLECHECK continued at his slow pace. "And remember, alias and cover are forms of deception. The best deceptions are built on a kernel of truth. So don't say you're a nuclear scientist if you know nothing about nuclear science."

The image on the whiteboard switched from the map of Ivanistan to a close up of a man and woman. "Here's the scenario. You will be preparing for an afternoon tea at the home of Mr. and Mrs. Vinic Brenjovic, natives of Ivanistan. A self-made millionaire and avid supporter of the arts, Mr. Brenjovic is devoted to advancing young Ivanistan artists, writers and poets. He and his wife host social events, like art shows and teas, bringing together high-ranking government officials and young artists."

MOLECHECK handed each recruit a sealed envelope. "At this party, you will practice the first step of the agent recruitment cycle: spotting and assessing. Your target's information is inside. Your mission is to make contact. Start a conversation, elicit some information and make arrangements to see the contact again. No one will suspect you of being a spy, unless you totally blow it by not knowing your cover."

Looking directly at Tex, MOLECHECK said, "I suggest you study and prepare for this party. It will be the first major test of your abilities, although some recruits won't even make it to the party. Fail and your spy days are over."

He placed a map of the underground tunnels that led back to the main camp on the table. Lee and Audrey ripped open their envelopes. Tex just stared at his.

"You'll find PUZZLE-GIRL in the classroom next door," MOLECHECK said.

Tex clenched his jaw. This was not what he expected. Meeting agents in the dark of night after slipping away from the bad guys with guns and dogs. YES. Bonding with some wannabe girl spy, no way. He was mentally flipping through his options when the bell rang releasing the recruits for lunch.

A green phone in the corner rang. MOLECHECK took the call, speaking in a hushed voice.

Lee pulled his biometric ID from his pocket. "Ready to explore the tunnels?"

"Later," Tex said. "I need to talk to MOLECHECK." He would end this partner business before it got started. Partnerships didn't go well for him. He wasn't letting anything get in the way of being a spy.

The second MOLECHECK hung up the phone, Tex started in. "Sir, I understand with Jennifer gone, Alpha team is one short. But I think I'm ready to work this tea party gig by myself." Tex crossed his arms. "No need to bring in an outsider, if you know what I mean."

MOLECHECK's eyes crinkled as he chuckled. He jumped up, giving Tex a slap on the back as he grabbed his canvas bag. Tex grinned. He knew MOLECHECK would get that he was different and could handle things on his own.

MOLECHECK paused in the doorway. "You don't need to be afraid of PUZZLE-GIRL. I'm confident you can hold your own."

What? MOLECHECK disappeared through the door a moment before a girl with brown curls stepped in, causing Tex's horror to multiply.

"Ready to meet?" Ria Santos marched over to Tex, her hand extended. "I thought we could start working on this right away."

"You're PUZZLE-GIRL?" Tex said to his LFP.

"The one and only," she said, her crazy hair flying.

Why did he have to be paired with her? She never stopped talking and thought she had all the answers. As he pushed past Ria, something on her wrist caught the pocket of his jacket. He pushed forward, but she came along with him, tugging on his favorite leather jacket.

"Wait a sec." Ria said, untangling her charm bracelet. "You're stuck with me COW-BOY, so you might as well deal with it."

Tex frowned. She was beyond annoying.

"We can work during lunch," Ria said, her curls bouncing around her. "I know a secret way into the mess hall."

Of course she did.

— • — • • • — • • • — — • — — — — — • •

Memo for the Record
Date/Time: 22 JUN/1910Z
To: CONTROL
From: MOLECHECK
Re: Alpha team

Initial assessment of Alpha team is positive, but with several reservations.

COW-BOY may be too much of a loner to work in the team environment necessary for real-world operations. I have paired him with PUZZLE-GIRL from Kappa to test his ability to deal with an equally strong personality and share decision-making.

MIND-READER may be too timid to seize opportunities and to impose her will on agents. The key challenge for her will be the recruitment exercise.

LAB-MAN is very impressive in a quiet way. Focused, detail oriented, shows strong critical thinking, and works well with everyone. He is the strongest of the three, but may lack the self-confidence needed to complete the program.

8

Codenames and Consequences

Lee leaned against the wall, his shoes on the blue line, ears trained on the sound of Tex and Ria arguing all the way down the corridor. He felt sorry for Tex. He wished they'd been paired together instead. MOLECHECK said the teams would constantly shift. Lee hoped it would happen before the two of them killed each other. As he waited for Audrey, who had gone looking for a real Band-Aid, Lee was hoping to run into Tex. Instead he found Marvin Ames grinning at him.

"What's your code name? Mine's EAGLE-EYES."

Lee pushed his glasses up on his nose and looked away. EAGLE-EYES? That was an odd name. Was there something unusual about Marvin's vision? LAB-MAN suggested he was a scientist. Or a nerd.

He wanted to ask why Marvin was spying on them, but he could hear Ria coming closer. Lee was not about to be caught talking to Tex's number one and number two LFP.

"Wanna see what I found?"

"I gotta go." Hands in his pocket, head down, eyes on the blue line, Lee turned to walk away.

Marvin's knobby-knees knocked alongside him. "It's an Indian Head nickel. I found it in the grass outside the bunkhouse." Marvin shoved the coin in front of Lee. "It's really rare. Want it?"

Lee stopped and looked at Marvin. In his experience, no one gave things away. "What do you want for it?" Lee kept his hands shoved deep in his pockets.

"Nothing. Well, maybe you'd let me hang out with you and Tex sometimes. Friends?"

Lee took the coin and turned it over in his hand. On one side there was the profile of an American Indian and on the other side, an American bison. The date embossed on the coin read 1912. Lee had never seen a real Indian Head nickel, except in books. But Einstein had. What would be the mathematical odds of Einstein having carried this one in his pocket? Remote, but theoretically possible. Lee smiled. Maybe Tex was wrong. Marvin wasn't such a bad kid after all.

"Thanks." Lee continued down the blue line. To his relief, Marvin didn't follow.

Audrey was waiting for him at the corner where the blue line met the red. She looked anxious. He knew exactly how she felt. What she needed was a good laugh. He took his new coin and flipped it in the air, catching it not with his hands, but on his forehead, like a seal.

"Aaarrff, Aaarrff," he barked, clapping his hands over his head. He glanced at her. She stared at him like he was a rabid animal. So much for his friends finding him funny. He dropped the coin into his hand and held it out to her. "It's a rare nickel from 1912."

"You're going to have to offer a lot more money than that to make up for being late."

"I'm here, so what's wrong?" Lee pocketed the coin.

"Wrong? Didn't you hear anything MOLECHECK said? We have to learn about a country that doesn't really exist. And become people who don't really exist. And we have to go back to camp where other kids do exist. Now we're late, and we're going to be in trouble—"

"If we don't exist, how can we be in trouble?" Lee said, trying to work through Audrey's logic.

Audrey stopped speaking and blinked. "Oh."

Lee wished his worries could be calmed that easily. He knew he existed and could prove it scientifically. MOLECHECK definitely suggested a cause-and-effect relationship between breaking rules and facing consequences. Lee wished MOLECHECK had been clearer about the consequences.

— · — · · · — · · · — — — · — — — — — · ·

Memo for the Record
Date/Time: 22 JUN/2000Z
From: Security
To: CONTROL
Re: Counter Intelligence Alert – MOLE Investigation

We successfully confiscated the toothbrush of possible imposter for additional testing. This was difficult, with the operation aborted several times. Subject is compulsive about oral hygiene and carries her toothbrush with her.

Saliva sample does not match file sample. Either the file sample is corrupted or subject is an imposter.

Options: (A) Interrogate subject; (B) Continue to monitor; (C) Remove subject from Camp.

Recommendation: Interrogation

9

Short-Term Memory Loss

The next week passed in a flash for Audrey. Half the time she spent in camp pretending to be a regular camper. The other half in spy school. As she walked the blue line with Lee, Audrey decided her initial fears were simply an overreaction.

Week one had been devoted to cover, alias and memorizing everything about the mythical Ivanistan to get ready for their first spy meeting. MOLECHECK gave each of them a dossier on their alias identity—who they were pretending to be in Ivanistan. That was easy: Lena Rose, ballerina, exchange student. Audrey was more intrigued by her contact. The dossier didn't include many details beyond his name, profession as a photographer and the fact that he was born in Ivanistan. Audrey wondered what he looked like. Photographers were artistic and sensitive, like her. She was sure she'd like him. She'd find out soon enough; the Brenjovic's tea party was in a week.

Audrey was ready to move on to this week's new spy skill: impersonal communications. She and Lee had spent the last two hours in the Commo Lab learning how to pass notes or small packages without being seen.

"The brush passes would be easier if you had bigger pockets," Lee complained.

Audrey laughed. She fingered the slit pocket on her double ruffled skirt, a quarter of the size of Lee's cargo pockets. Audrey had no problem slipping her notes into Lee's pocket as she brushed past him. It must be a sign. Her grandmamma said coming to this camp was Audrey's destiny. This wasn't like at home. If she had questions, all she had to do was ask to get answers. She could relax.

"Okay, so my pocket is small, but what's your excuse for the bad palm passes?"

"Sweaty palms?" Lee said.

They both laughed. More than half of the notes they tried to pass during a handshake, from palm to palm, ended up on the floor. They were both pretty good at swapping identical bags without anyone noticing.

As they turned down the next hallway, they walked right into a checkpoint. Two barrel-shaped trashcans barred the way. A man with the words SECURITY on his cap leaned on one of the cans, clipboard in hand. Beyond him was the door to their homeroom. There was no avoiding him.

A light switched on. Audrey shielded her eyes.

"Who goes?" the man demanded.

"Audrey. Audrey Rochais," she said, panic rising. Had they gone into an off-limits red corridor by mistake?

Lee remained silent.

"Come forward and present your identification," the man ordered.

Her identification? Did he want her badge? Audrey stepped forward, fumbling for the plastic identification badge around her neck all recruits were required to wear while in the secret facility.

"Your Ivanistan resident card."

Audrey's fingers froze as she realized her mistake. This checkpoint was Ivanistan, not spy school. The man at the barrier was none other than Eric Little. Audrey had a run-in with him on the first night and every day afterwards. It felt like he was always trying to trip her up. In Ivanistan, she lived in alias. She was not Audrey Rochais. But who was she? Her memory failed her. Instead, MOLECHECK's advice rang in her ears. *Change the subject. Create a diversion. Get in control of threatening situations.* Instinctively, Audrey rammed against Lee, who bumped into the barrier. The barrel hit the spot light, which teetered on its base.

Eric Little dropped the clipboard to catch the lamp before it fell.

"Sorry," Audrey said.

"Identification cards," Eric demanded.

"Here's mine," Lee said.

The light switched off and Lee handed Eric his Ivanistan identification card, which gave his name as Tom Kirk.

Eric held the card and made a show of comparing Lee's face to the picture. "What is your relationship," Eric demanded.

"Ah, friends," Lee said.

"And her name?" With a sharp point of his finger, Eric made it clear he wanted the answer from Lee, not Audrey.

"Ahhhh—"

"Friends and you don't know her name?"

"I'm Lena Rose," Audrey blurted out, the name popping out of the dark recess of her brain.

Eric Little's eyes burned into Audrey as he sneered.

"Thought you said your name was Audrey. Identification card. Now." He thrust out his hand.

Audrey pulled the card out, hand shaking. "No," she protested. "I said, "Howdy." It's a greeting in English. You don't use it in Ivanistan?"

Eric held the card, but did not take his eyes off of Audrey. She tried not to squirm.

"Where do you live?" he demanded. Audrey fumbled through her street address, misplacing several of the digits. Lee claimed he just moved to Ivanistan and hadn't memorized it yet.

"What are you doing in this part of Ivanistan?"

"Heading home," Audrey said.

"And you?" Eric demanded from Lee.

"I'm with her," Lee said to his shoes, jamming his hands into his pockets.

"I could arrest you both for suspicious behavior." Eric slapped the clipboard against the metal can, making Audrey and Lee jump.

A small canister popped out of Lee's pocket and rolled across the floor. They had been using the old film container to hide messages during the brush pass practice session.

Eric's foot stopped the container from rolling past the checkpoint. He popped the cap, and removed a tightly rolled piece of paper.

Meet you tomorrow, same place, and time. Parole: Tuna. Counter Parole: Fresh Bass. Audrey swallowed. Parol and counter-parole were spy terms for recognition signals, codes that identify the recruit to the agent and signal that everything is secure.

Eric wet his lips. He glowered at Audrey and then Lee. Audrey tried not to fidget. Silence. Then voices echoed down the corridor. Ria Santos and Hannah Martin appeared around the corner.

"The Murder Board is going to love this," Eric said pocketing the note and the container. "Go," he motioned to Audrey and Lee. Then he flipped on the light, blinding Ria and Hannah.

"Who goes?" was the last thing Audrey heard as she and Lee escaped into the safety of the homeroom. Before she could drop her backpack, Lee had a bag of marshmallows in his hands. Brain food, he called them.

"Murder board?" he said with marshmallows stuffed in both cheeks.

"He's trying to scare us." Audrey poked at the white cube.

"J.J. from Omega team was sent to the Murder Board yesterday," Lee whispered in the empty room. "He was caught in the red corridor, near the instructors' offices," Lee said. "I think the kid from Iota who ratted on him was also eliminated. Both of their bunks were empty this morning."

"Charlie?" Her fingers reached for the round medallion hanging around her neck. On one side was the profile of a lady wearing a cap with an eagle's head and feathers, with FREEDOM printed boldly around the curved edge. The Liberty Bell was on the back. It had been awarded to her grandmamma for her brave actions saving American soldiers during World War II.

"Guess the Murder Board doesn't like rule breakers or snitches."

Lee groaned. "I'm not going to make it. I know I'm next."

"You didn't mess up at the check point." Audrey flung her chair around, no longer caring what the camera captured. "I thought we were done with cover lessons. Why did I tell him my real name?"

"I don't think he gave either of us gold stars."

"We need to be better prepared next time." Audrey said as she rose from her chair to prowl around the room. "Or our bunks will be the next empty ones."

"Why do I have to know this stuff?" Lee's fingers searched for the bag of marshmallows. "I want to invent new spy technologies, not play make believe."

Audrey gave the top of his spiky head a cautious pat, like she might wake a sleepy porcupine. She liked working with Lee. "You know, my grandmamma was an actress and a wartime spy for the French Resistance. She said I'd discover my destiny here. I didn't know it was a spy camp. Maybe your parents sent you here for the same reason."

Lee looked at Audrey. "There is no way my parents are spies. They thought this was a science camp. My destiny, according to my parents, is college at MIT on a full scholarship. Dad says the only way it'll happen is if I get a personality and become interesting to recruiters. I don't think you're allowed to put spy school on the college application."

"MOLECHECK said we couldn't tell anyone."

"That's the problem. You don't know what it's like in my family. My dad's expectations are like laws. Break them and be disowned. I'm expected to become a famous scientist and bring the family honor. But now I have a chance to be a spy and invent cool things like that kid who saved us from a global computer meltdown. Only I can't tell them. They'll just think I'm a loser." Lee's eyes gleamed behind his glasses and then clouded. "Maybe it's my destiny to be a loser. I didn't think spying would be this hard."

"I don't think spying's going to be the hard part. Lying about being a spy is the problem."

"You mean living under cover?"

"My mom would not approve of me lying to her. At home, I can get away with almost anything, but not lying. She catches me every time, even the littlest, itsy-bitsy lie."

"If you don't tell her anything, you're not technically lying," Lee said.

"Maybe." Audrey suspected her mom would not buy any technicalities.

"What would your grandmother say?" Lee asked.

Audrey fingered her medallion. "She would say there are different kinds of lies. Bad ones to cover up evil and good ones to protect people."

"I agree with your grandmother. Maybe you can ask her if she has some advice for me?"

"She passed away last September." Audrey stretched her arms above her head to force the ache in her heart away. She curved left in an arch and then right. What would her grandmamma do? She'd treat it like learning a role in a play and she'd make it a game. "Maybe we're taking all of this too seriously. MOLECHECK encouraged us to have fun with the exercises."

"Yeah, it's just an experiment. Take 35 kids." Lee held the half empty bag of marshmallows. "Torture them." He squished the bag between his hands flattening the puffs. "Terrify them." Lee shook the bag viciously. "And beat them into submission to see what they do." Then he slammed the bag down on the table three times. "Are we having fun yet?" Lee tossed Audrey the mashed mallows.

Audrey smiled. Lee reminded her of how passionate her grandmamma would become when taking on a new role in a play.

"Not an experiment, a play. That's it." Audrey sprang from her chair and did four graceful pirouettes. "We have to become the characters, and then they can't surprise us."

Lee gave an exasperated sigh. "Okay, but only if you agree that we use scientific methodology."

"Like what," Audrey asked knowing it didn't matter. Lee would play along. She could feel it.

— • — • • • — • • • — — — • — — — — — • •

Memo for the Record
Date/Time: 29 JUN/0400Z
To: CONTROL
Info: MOLECHECK
From: SARGENT
Re: Alpha team - Recruit LAB-MAN

Recruit LAB-MAN is falling behind in PT. Part of the
problem is his sedentary lifestyle. He is not involved in
any sports. More problematic is his attitude and
consumption of junk food. Recommend counseling and
stern message that PT is not optional, but an essential
part of the Junior Spy Program. He has one week to
improve running, sit-ups and pushup scores. If he fails, he
should be selected out.

⑩

The Writings on the Wall

Lee leaned over and carefully aligned his right eye with the microscope eyepiece. He turned the focus button until the image sharpened. Through the microscope's lens, he could see a microdot on the celluloid film, invisible to the naked eye.

Excitement replaced the feeling of dread that dominated Lee after days of forced runs and interrogations at roadblocks. He was finally doing something he was good at. He knew he was close to disqualification after failing the timed run. After 15 days, the body count on the teams was dropping. He was going to have to step it up. Literally.

Today, Alpha team was assigned to LAB 2D05, the Commo Lab, with Instructor DASH to learn another spy skill: secret writing. Lee liked DASH right away, with his white lab coat and selection of pens, brushes and pick-like tools in his breast pocket. DASH spoke Lee's language, the language of microscopes, chemicals and atoms.

DASH told them to pair with someone from a different team. Counting heads, he saw Omega was down to two members. Kappa still had three. Last night, Brian Babbitt from Theta team disappeared. His bunk was empty and all his personal gear gone. All MOLECHECK would say this morning was he had been eliminated. Lee didn't like the word "eliminated." It sounded too much like "terminated." Too permanent.

Ria and Hannah stuck together like an ionic compound, ignoring DASH's request to mix up the teams. Tex refused to share his table when Marvin tried to sit down. So Lee ended up at the back table with the weasel. That put Audrey with the two remaining members of Omega: Brenton Meyers and Connor Philips. Lee noticed they didn't seem to mind sitting on either side of Audrey, competing for her attention.

"Time to move from invisible inks to microdots," DASH said. He leaned against a display case at the front of the room. "Tomorrow, you'll be writing a coded message to your agent in Ivanistan and concealing it inside one of these." DASH pointed to several items inside the display case. From a distance, one looked like a dead rat and the other a cow pie.

Lee had already mastered making invisible inks out of lemon juice. The acid was the key because it left invisible traces on the paper after the juice dried. Lee sprinkled the paper with water one more time and watched the acid trail re-emerge, revealing his favorite Einstein quote: "The secret to creativity is knowing how to hide your sources."

As he grabbed his microscope, he noticed everyone had moved on to the next assignment except for Marvin. He was still working with the invisible inks. Lee made a show of rubbing his eyes while watching Marvin wrap two of his notes in another sheet of paper and slide the paper into his camp-issued backpack. It was identical to the one belonging to Lee.

Tex called Marvin trouble. Lee agreed. He'd met too many Marvins in his short life. They were worse than bullies who took pleasure out of beating you up in front of your friends. Kids like Marvin attacked you when you weren't looking and didn't leave a trail. They were the teachers' pets by day but flesh-eating bacteria after school. Lee decided to keep an eye on Marvin, if only for his own protection.

"The microdot you have under your scope uses old-fashioned film," DASH said.

Lee studied the long out-of-date technology with acute fascination. Without the microscope, it looked like a speck of dirt on the white paper. Under the scope, Lee saw a page-length letter typed in Cyrillic letters. Russian, he guessed.

"During the Cold War our Soviets agents used microdots like this one to send messages."

"But you still use microdots, don't you?" Hannah asked.

"Yes. Computers and digital imaging have replaced film and glue. The concept remains the same. Agents still need ways to communicate in secret."

Tex frowned at Hannah. "Do we get to use this stuff, or just talk about it?"

"Patience, COW-BOY," DASH said. "Do you know what micro printing is?"

Tex shook his head.

"Micro printing and microdots are both used as security measures. Micro printing, however, is easier to read. Have you ever looked at a $10 bill under a magnifying glass?" Tex shook his head. DASH took a bill from his wallet and invited him to examine it.

"Wow, these lines aren't really lines," Tex said. "It says THE UNITED STATES OF AMERICA."

"Cool! Move over so I can see." Marvin pushed to the front of the room with the rest of the class.

Lee hung back. He reached down, grabbed his pack and dropped it next to Marvin's stool then he kicked Marvin's backpack under his own.

"You can do this on your own," DASH continued. "Write a message and then change the font size so you reduce each letter to what looks like a dot. Copy the dots into another document—something boring, say—and use the dots as periods. Print the document, and using a magnifying glass, you'll be able to read the message."

"The message couldn't be very long," Brenton said.

"Less than 10 characters if you want it to look like a period. Plus, it's not very secure. Professionals use a different method of taking a digital image of a secret note, reducing it to the size of a pixel, then hiding it inside another digital image. In essence, a picture hidden inside another picture."

DASH handed each of them a photograph of an English Sheepdog. According to the instructions, a secret message was hidden in a pixel somewhere in the fur covering the dog's left eye. Sweet Einstein! A pixel? Lee owned a digital camera. It wasn't an expensive one, only 3.1 megapixels. Each image contained 3,145,728 colored dots, or pixels. You'd have to enlarge each of the millions of pixels to check for secret messages or pictures. Even knowing the message was hidden near the eye didn't help much. Talk about looking for a needle in a virtual haystack. Whoever invented this was brilliant. If Lee made it through spy school, this is what he wanted to do. Be the "Q," inventor of spy gadgets, to Tex's James Bond.

DASH headed to the door. "I'll check back in on you in an hour. If you finish early, read the lesson on concealment devices and check out the examples in the display case," DASH said. "You will be making your own tomorrow."

The flash of a camera blinded Lee. "I'll start the photos," Marvin said. "You can do the embedding work. Then we'll switch." Marvin started snapping pictures of each member of the class, along with the equipment in the room. He took a lot more pictures than Lee thought necessary. He toyed with the idea of sneaking a look inside Marvin's pack while he was busy, but decided it was too risky. He went to work instead preparing the base image in which he would hide Marvin's photos.

"COW-BOY?"

Lee looked up to see Hannah walking toward Tex.

She stared at him, raising her eyes slightly to peer through thick lashes before smiling. Lee wondered if Tex found the eye thing odd too.

"What do you want?" Tex said sharply, without taking his eyes off of his computer.

"I was wondering if you could show me how you embed the files," Hannah said. "I must be doing something wrong because I keep getting an error message." She held out a paper to show Tex and batted her eyes.

Lee shifted for a better view. Girls asked him for help at school all the time, but not like that. They made it clear they just wanted the information and then left. Fast.

"Ask PUZZLE-GIRL, she's the know-it-all." Tex's eyes remained on the screen in front of him.

"We're stuck," Hannah smiled and fixed her gaze on him. "Please?"

Tex looked at her; his jaw set hard.

Lee pushed up his glasses. Watch out Einstein. Chemical reaction in the works.

"What are you trying to pull PUZZLE-GIRL?" Tex snapped, glaring over at Ria.

Hannah grabbed her papers and fled, sending the stool crashing to the floor. Audrey shrieked, knocking over her stool too. Hannah rushed out of the lab, her face bright red. To Lee's surprise, Marvin grabbed his backpack and hurried after her.

Tex kept his eyes on the screen. His ability to ignore his surroundings ended seconds later when Ria shoved her face into his.

"Why are you being such a jerk?" she demanded.

"I've got you figured out. You think you're so smart; you get NIGHT-WIND to do your dirty work and steal my answers. I'm not falling for it."

Ria's black eyes were on fire. Lee had never seen her so worked up. "See if I help you when you need it." Ria stormed out of the lab, leaving Tex with his fists balled, looking like he wanted to fight.

"Easy," Lee said. "You can't let a girl get you kicked out of spy school." Lee grabbed Marvin's backpack and pushed Tex toward the door.

"Let's see what Marvin is hiding." Lee reached inside for the papers Marvin had stashed away. Instead he pulled out a handful of empty M&M wrappers.

Tex gave him a '*what gives*' look.

This was his pack, not Marvin's. The little snake had switched them back.

— • — • • • — • • • — — • — — — — • •

Memo for the Record
Date/Time: 30 JUN/1530Z
To: All Homeroom Instructors
From: CONTROL
RE: Recruit Elimination

Epsilon recruit GREEN-SPOTTER and Iota recruit CODE-DUDE have been selected out for unsuitability. These two recruits practiced poor security discussing classified spy school activities in the vicinity of unauthorized campers.

Request Epsilon and Iota homeroom instructors clear out their safes and destroy their files.

All homeroom instructors review security practices with recruits.

White Chalk and Black Marks

Audrey clutched the white chalk in the palm of her right hand. She was nervous, but a good nervous, when she saw the metal trashcan bolted to the concrete slab. The trees and the curve of the path blocked the view of the trashcan from the Assembly Area. She could hear the voices of the campers but no one could see what she was about to do: put down a signal that the dead drop site was loaded.

"Kinda cool, us being spies and everything, huh?"

Startled, Audrey twirled around to find Marvin half-hidden in the bushes.

She looked around for anything else hidden in the bushes, like a camera, or Eric Little. "We're not supposed to, you know, talk about it. And I, uh, shouldn't be seen with you right now."

"I've tried to catch you after homeroom, but you're always with your team."

Audrey nodded, thinking of all the times she'd seen Marvin's nose pressed against the homeroom window, signaling to her. A couple of times she tried to catch him after class, but Tex chased him away. Sometimes Tex could be mean, like when he called Marvin a weasel to his face. What would Tex say if he caught them talking? And how long had Marvin been watching her?

"It's okay, I already checked to make sure the coast was clear."

"Did you see me—?"

"Put down your dead drop. Yeah, but I won't tell anyone," Marvin said.

Audrey silently groaned and reached for her necklace. "I guess that's why you're codename is EAGLE-EYES. You see everything. I can only read people's minds." She leaned in toward Marvin to sense if he was telling her the truth. "If I can see the whites of their eyes."

Marvin blinked several times and backed away.

"Kidding." Audrey laughed.

"Oh." Marvin laughed too, but it sounded a bit too high and lasted too long.

Sensing she'd gone too far, Audrey began to twist the chain. If she made Marvin mad, would he change his mind and tell the instructors that Audrey had failed the most important step of putting down a dead drop? She gave him her brightest smile. "Maybe we can talk tomorrow. I've got something I have to do right now and thanks for not telling anyone what you saw...or didn't see." She took a step around Marvin.

"Wait." He held out a small wrapped package. "I made this for you."

Audrey took the small bundle. "Really? Thanks."

Inside was a piece of wood, the message hand-carved. *Nicest Girl I've Ever Known.* So much for reading minds— she hadn't seen that one coming. Feeling the blood rush to her face, she kept her head down to hide her confusion. When she did look up, she saw Marvin only an instant before he disappeared around the bend. Flustered by her own feelings, she tried to force herself to concentrate on her mission.

To be certified, she had to show she could handle an already-recruited agent, step four of the agent recruitment cycle. MOLECHECK had given her TINKER. Her assignment was to guide the agent to steal secrets for her without getting caught. Audrey groaned. So much for following the instructions.

MOLECHECK told her that face-to-face meetings with TINKER would be too dangerous. He would never be able to explain meeting with an American. TINKER's boss was a suspicious man and would report him to the police.

Audrey would have to handle him using impersonal communication methods, specifically dead drops. She was to leave hidden notes for him without being seen.

She was proud of the hair brush concealment device she had made. Hannah gave her the idea. Audrey was surprised Hannah would even talk to her after how Tex treated her the other day. But when Audrey needed help, Hannah was the first to offer ideas that had nothing to do with vermin or disgusting animal droppings.

She found what she needed in the disguise lab, an old brush with many missing bristles. No one would pick it up, other than TINKER. And if some curious camper did and found the paper rolled inside the hollow handle, he still wouldn't be any wiser because Audrey had written her message in invisible ink. The real risk was to be seen putting it down. She did dozens of practice drops during the week to perfect dropping the brush down the side of her leg, using her body to screen the falling brush while still getting it into the target drop area.

At exactly 12:25 pm, (12 and 25 being two of her lucky numbers), Audrey dropped the concealment device for TINKER into a small hollow spot by the northern-most footing of Ivanistan's watchtower. Except for Marvin spotting her, the drop went perfectly.

Could she trust Marvin and put down the signal that it was safe for TINKER to retrieve the drop?

According to the file, TINKER worked in the Ivanistan Harbor Masters office. He knew every ship that came into and left the Ivanistan harbor. Audrey asked him if the Ivanistan government was sending cargo shipments to its warring neighbors, and if so, if there were weapons in those shipments. Ivanistan was supposed to be neutral. MOLECHECK said the U.S. was getting intelligence that Michaldom was receiving weapons from Ivanstan. If true, Samvia might retaliate and attack Ivanistan. If it wasn't true, someone might be trying to deceive the leaders of Samvia in order to trick them into attacking Ivanistan. TINKER was well placed to find out the truth.

Now all that was left was to signal that the drop was ready to be picked up. Audrey rolled the piece of chalk in her fist so only the tip stuck out. She double-checked to make sure no one was around. It was 12:30 pm. (Thirty was another one of her lucky numbers.) Should she do it? She believed Marvin. He won't say anything, but she also sensed something else from him. A confused worry, a pressure on him, or a—

"AUUUUUUUDREY"

Feet pounded the path. Audrey turned in a panic. She rolled the chalk in her hand before tossing it into the bushes. Her mind raced. What was her cover story?

Lee burst around the corner, sweat pouring down his forehead. His shirt was soaked. "AUUUD—" Lee stopped yelling as soon as he saw her.

"Shush!" Audrey looked to see if anyone was following him. "You scared me."

"M-O-L-E-C-H-E-C-K wants to see us." Lee's words came out between broken breaths.

Audrey's thoughts flew to Marvin. No, it wasn't possible.

"We can take the tunnel behind the boy's bunkhouse," Lee said.

MOLECHECK was waiting for them in the empty homeroom. He instructed them to take a seat at the ops table, but he did not join them.

The color drained from Audrey. MOLECHECK avoided all eye contact.

"You are aware one of the basic rules of spying is trust. You must trust those you pick to work with. You have to trust the team you rely on, and everyone around you has to know you are as good as your word."

MOLECHECK took a handkerchief out of his pants pocket and wiped the sweat running off his bald spot. Audrey looked at Lee whose magnified eyes were blinking abnormally fast. He shook his head, confused.

"We had a first at spy school yesterday. Your written report on the political situation in Ivanistan was similar to the one presented by Kappa team. Perhaps it is a coincidence, but the Murder Board will convene tonight, and decide about your future as recruits.

"Murder Board?" Audrey squeaked. "Cheating?" Her head swam. She felt light-headed and had trouble breathing. Not the dead drop. What report was MOLECHECK talking about?

"Recruits don't have the right to argue their case before the Board. You can submit a written explanation, but the Board's decision is final." MOLECHECK mopped his brow. "Your only hope is to tell the truth. All of it."

"But we didn't do anything wrong," Lee said.

"If you are selected out, you must accept the consequences of your actions."

Consequences? Audrey twisted the chain of her necklace and thought about the other recruits who were terminated. One day they were here at camp, the next day gone without a trace. Did they let you pack your gear and send you home or did they dump you and your stuff someplace never to be found?

"I suggest you use this time to prepare your explanation." MOLECHECK left without even a good-bye as he closed the door behind him.

— • — • • • — • • • — — • — — — — — • •

Memo for the Record
Date/Time: 5 JUL/1800Z
To: Performance Review Board Members
From: CONTROL
RE: Agenda for Meeting

The PRB will convene at 2000 hours to review the cases of six recruits (files attached). Please note the serious security concerns of one of these cases. Security officer TRAIL will give a counter intelligence briefing to PRB members, which is TOP SECRET, Code Word-controlled. The information is not; repeat not, to be shared with instructor staff.

Operation Burn Bag

Lee lifted his head off the ops table at the sound of the door opening. It was Tex.

"Did I miss nap time?"

"Go away." Lee groaned.

"What's going on?"

"MOLECHECK said our report was exactly like one from Kappa team," Audrey sniffled.

"The Murder Board is meeting tomorrow. We're going to get kicked out. If they don't kill us first." Lee planted his face back on the table. At this point, he felt getting killed the better of the two options. Then he wouldn't have to admit he was a total failure.

"Get a grip L-Man. Someone set you up."

"Set us up? Why?" Audrey said.

"Someone wants you out of the program," Tex said.

"Eric Little," Audrey choked out. "Every time something bad happens, Eric is around. Like it's his personal mission to catch me making mistakes."

"The counselor?" Tex looked at Lee in disbelief.

"I saw Eric in here last night. I came back to check that I had locked and spun off the safe."

"What was he doing?" Tex's eyes narrowed.

"He said he had to set up a PowerPoint presentation for MOLECHECK. Ria told me that Hannah overhead the other instructors talking about him. He was involved in some operation that went bad. He was pulled from the team and sent back here to help with training instead. Did you know his codename is BULLDOG?"

"BULLDOG? That doesn't mean he's taking his anger out on the recruits by getting them eliminated. Nope," Tex said, shaking his head. "That dog don't hunt."

"Ria said Hannah told her Eric was picking on her too. Sound familiar?" Audrey didn't know how, but she wasn't going to let Eric get away with it.

While Audrey and Tex argued about Eric, Lee shoved his hands deep into the pocket of his long cargo shorts. Was his spy career about to end? Didn't he finish running the mile in PT this morning under 15 minutes, a personal best? Better yet, he invented the coolest concealment device: a silicon wad of chewing gum, sticky and gross.

Inside, he hid a scrap of lined paper, blank except for a microdot hidden on the top line. DASH said it was the best any recruit had made.

Maybe he hadn't performed well on some of the exercises, but he was not a cheater. Sure, he'd replicated others' experiments in the lab, but that was different. Replication is part of the scientific process. Claiming someone else's work? Never. He searched for possible explanations as his fingers felt something wedged in the corner of his pocket. The coin.

"Hey, check this out." Lee tossed the coin to Tex, who wasn't expecting it. The coin hit the floor, after bouncing off of Audrey's sneakers.

"Marvin said it's from 1912." Lee felt stupid the second the words slipped out.

"The rodent gave you this?" Tex picked it up and examined it.

"It's really rare."

"Are you still playing with that thing?" Audrey said.

Lee blushed, remembering his failed attempt to get Audrey to laugh.

"Sure is rare. They didn't start making these until 1913." Tex put the coin between his teeth and bit down.

"Hungry?" Lee wondered if he was trying to be funny.

"It's hollow." Tex took a small penknife from his pocket and cut into the coin.

"Hey, don't break it." Lee grabbed for the coin.

Tex body-blocked Lee as the coin cracked open. "Lookie here. A miniature battery and some wire. Where would old EAGLE-EYES have gotten one of those?"

Oh Einstein. How could he be so stupid to not consider outside contamination, the most basic control for every scientific experiment?

"It's a bug." Tex dropped it on the floor and smashed it to bits with the heel of his cowboy boot.

"That cockroach! Now we know how he stole our report. We've got to tell MOLECHECK," Lee said.

"No! Remember what happen to the kid who ratted out J.J?" Audrey said "Gone. Disappeared. I don't believe Marvin would have done this. Someone planted the coin on him, and he just shared. Eric could have given it to him. Eric's a trained spy."

"If we don't tell MOLECHECK about the coin and EAGLE-EYES, the Murder Board will eliminate us," Lee said.

"Maybe someone set up EAGLE-EYES too? We could ask him where he got it." Audrey poked the coin bits. "He might tell me."

"I could get him to confess." Tex smashed his fist into the palm of his hand.

"EAGLE-EYES would rat you out as a bully." Lee bent over and picked up the pieces before Audrey scattered them everywhere, pocketing them with a plan to examine how they worked later. It bothered Lee that Audrey was standing up for Marvin. He could tell Audrey liked Marvin by the way she smiled at him, but why?

"What if we could show how we came up with our research? That's how a scientist would do it. We wouldn't be snitching on anyone, just proving our work was original." Lee said.

"I guess that could work too," Audrey said. "I still think—"

"Did either of you keep your drafts?" Tex interrupted.

"I put mine in the burn bag last night," Lee said.

"Me too." Audrey's shoulders slumped.

Lee scanned the room. There was not a loose piece of paper on a desk or burn bag to be seen. "We're sunk."

"Not yet. Looks like we need to execute an operation to infiltrate the incinerator room. Maybe the bags haven't been toasted." Tex headed for the door and then stopped.

"What's wrong?" Lee said to Tex when Audrey thudded into the back of him.

"I, uh, don't know where the incinerator room is," Tex admitted.

"Follow me," Lee said.

"How do you know?" Tex fell into step with Lee, as Audrey trailed behind.

"Found it by accident one day." Lee pushed forward in an effort to outpace Tex, not wanting to explain further.

Lee led them along the deserted corridor to the red line, the one area of spy school forbidden to recruits. The colored lines on the floor that seemed so confusing on the first day now seemed like a logical mapping system. Blue signified low security areas like the homerooms, gym and library. The green led to the labs. All they had been told was the second they passed through the double doors they would be violating Rule 53C.

As they stood on the threshold of breaking Rule 53C, Hannah rounded the corner. "I'd watch out if you're going that way." Hannah pointed at the doors. "I saw CONTROL headed for her office a minute ago."

"Thanks," Audrey gushed. "Of course, we wouldn't dream of going into the red area. That would be like mixing red with blue, and then we'd have purple. And, well, you can't have that."

Hannah stared at Audrey for a second, before fluttering her fingers at Tex as a wave good-bye and continuing along the blue line.

"That reminds me," Lee said. "What's our cover in case we get caught?"

Tex's face was flushed. "We're here to protest these false accusations. We need to deny everything."

Lee charted the route in his mind, hoping they wouldn't run into CONTROL. Then he pushed open the doors, leading them down the path of no return. He hoped he wasn't making a mistake. The law of outside contamination intervened before they had gone 25 steps.

"I need to talk to you." Marvin's voice rang out from around a corner.

The team froze against the wall.

"EAGLE-EYES," CONTROL said. "I already told you, the Murder Board will decide your case. This area is off-limits. I will escort you out."

Lee's fingers fumbled behind him feeling for a doorknob. It turned. "In here," he whispered. Crouching among shelves of office supplies, Lee listened to the sound of Marvin's footsteps pass by. The squeak of CONTROL's shoes started and faded away, like she was headed the other direction. A run-in with CONTROL would have been lethal.

Once he was sure the coast was clear, Lee continued down the red line, avoiding CONTROL's office, and a janitor, before reaching the incinerator room. The burn bags were piled high along the walls.

"We'll be here all night," Audrey whined.

"We need a system," Lee said. "We start with the bags by the door since they're probably the most recent. We'll work our way back toward the incinerator."

Tex grabbed the first bag and dumped it on the floor. Lee squatted next to him, sifting through reams of paper: handwritten notes, study sheets, draft reports, and lab sheets. Lee no longer cared about what his parents would say or the shame of being sent home for cheating. Only the papers in front of him mattered.

They worked in silence for the better part of an hour, broken only by a loud screech from Audrey. "Hey, who's putting peanut butter and jelly in the burn bags?" She waved a hand at Lee, fingers covered with brown and purple lumps.

"Well I'll be a monkey's uncle." Tex held a handful of bits of ripped paper. "This came from Kappa's bag. Someone didn't want the risk of anyone reading it."

"EAGLE-EYES's on Kappa," Lee said.

Lee cleared a space to assemble the pieces like a jigsaw puzzle.

"Let me help." Audrey's hot breath radiated on the back of Lee's neck. "The jumbly one goes over there." Audrey pointed to the left of Lee's pile.

"Aud, I can't think with you standing over me." Lee swatted her hand away. He could hear her sigh when she moved back to her pile in the corner.

Minutes ticked away. Lee's stomach rumbled while he considered the paper puzzle. "That's weird. It's part of a list or something. Names of campers and their backgrounds…home addresses…parents' names. I can't figure out what the rest means."

"Voila!" Audrey popped up from behind a stack of bags, holding a wad of papers in her hand. "I found some of my papers. These might be yours."

Lee left the paper puzzle to Tex and helped Audrey sort through the papers. The proof they hadn't cheated was there in black and white. As he knelt down, a sudden flash of light caught Lee's attention. High in the corner where the wall met the ceiling, a metal mesh plate covered a two square inch area. The corridor may have been empty, but Lee suspected the area behind the metal mesh was not.

— • — • • • — • • • — — • — — — — • •

Memo for the Record
Date/Time: 5 JUL/0330Z
To: ALL INSTRUCTORS
From: CONTROL
RE: MURDER BOARD RESULTS

Review of Alpha team recruits LAB-MAN and MIND-READER and Kappa team recruits EAGLE-EYES and NIGHT-WIND for possible cheating found inconsistencies in the teams' stories, but no clear evidence to determine the culprit(s).

Normally, the Board would select out all four based on doubts about their integrity. However, given a related counterintelligence investigation (Top Secret, Code-Word-Controlled, Need-to-Know-Only Basis), the Board has decided it is more important to keep these recruits under 24/7 surveillance at this time. Elimination would make constant surveillance more difficult.

Instructors are requested to closely monitor the activities of these recruits, including possible indicators that they had known each other before arriving at Camp.

⓭
Social Butterflies

Audrey slammed her pack onto the homeroom table, causing both Tex and Lee to jump. She had not slept a wink, worrying that the Murder Board wouldn't believe them, only to find out the Murder Board had not only cleared both her and Lee, but also Marvin and Hannah too.

Audrey resented that the Murder Board didn't have to explain itself. It was like dealing with her mom. It was okay for her mom to question her and accuse her not doing or telling her things, but when Audrey's mom said she didn't want to talk about it, like anything to do with her father, whom Audrey had never met or even seen a picture of, those questions were against the rules. The rules should be the same for both sides.

"We had proof of our innocence. What did they have? Nothing!" Audrey shrieked.

"Why are you all bowed up?" Tex said.

"Nothing!!!"

"We've all been cleared. The why doesn't matter anymore? Maybe they have evidence none of us knows about," Lee said.

"Seriously?!" Audrey did three rapid turns, spinning like a Tasmanian Devil.

"You need to chill. The tea party is in a few hours," Lee said.

"Who cares about a stupid tea party?" Tex pranced up to Audrey, blowing kisses into the air. "Darling, sooo nice to seeee you. Whaaat a mahhvalouss dreeess. Have you triiied the finger sandwiches?"

"Ugh." She crossed her arms and plopped down in her chair. Lee was right, even though being calm was not an option. Social events were so awkward in the best of circumstances, when she knew who she was supposed to be. She was far more comfortable having conversations in her head than with strangers. She pulled out her study guide on Ivanistan. After surviving the cheating accusations, she could not risk getting thrown out for not knowing her operational environment inside and out.

At precisely 2:30 pm, MOLECHECK was waiting outside with a van and driver to take them to the party. "You all clean up quite nicely," he said as they climbed in. Mr. Corwin wore a dark navy blue tie with the emblem of Ivanistan: a black wild boar. It was the most conservative tie Audrey had seen him wear. Lee had slicked down his porcupine quills, making him looking a bit like an Asian Elvis, and Tex kept shifting in his seat and pulling at the tie around his neck. Tex told Audrey several times he had no interest in this "sissy charm school" stuff.

MOLECHECK reminded them this was a spot-and-assess exercise, and he stressed they had only one hour to find their contact. Their assignment was to collect additional biographical information on the target and arrange a follow-up meeting somewhere in Ivanistan. The other teams would be collecting counterintelligence to disrupt their operations. This was a competition, not a tea party.

The Brenjovic's house was in a gated part of Ivanistan. The house was framed with a row of large white pillars, and tightly trimmed boxwood hedges surrounded the massive front porch. Audrey could hear the sound of violins coming from inside.

"Welcome," Mr. and Mrs. Brenjovic said as they greeted each one of them. Audrey made sure to give a firm, but brief handshake. She noticed Mrs. Brenjovic wince when Tex grabbed her hand. Audrey glided through the entry, pausing to smell the lilies, and then entered the adjoining dining room. She breathed deeply, in and out like her ballet teacher recommended before stepping on stage, when something solid knocked her into the side table and sent a ceramic vase rolling.

"We're in." Lee smoothed back his hair.

Audrey righted the vase on the table, but it was too late to recover her confidence. "Thanks for ruining my entrance."

"Sorry. Must be low blood sugar or something. Let's eat." Before Audrey could stop him, Lee had filled a plate with tiny sandwiches and individual cakes from the buffet.

"We're working, remember. You need to find your contact, not eat."

"There." With a handful of food, Lee pointed across the dining room at a distinguished looking man in a three-piece suit. He carried a cane with a gold handle. "Kardi Krozac, the Chairman of the Ivanistan Council of Ministers." Lee jammed the cake into his mouth, sending chocolate sprinkles down the front of his jacket.

"How did you do that?"

"The eyes, always watching," Lee said.

Audrey patted the sprinkles off his clothes, grabbed his arm, and led him across the dining room. "MOLECHECK said we should make contact right away." They were a few steps away from Chairman Krozac when Marvin cut in.

"You look pretty," Marvin said to Audrey. "Can I get you something to drink?"

She could feel her cheeks burn. She hadn't told anyone Marvin had a crush on her. She was certain that he hadn't told the instructors about the dead drop because when she had gone back to put down the signal to tell TINKER it was safe to unload the dead drop, everything seemed okay. She had thought he was sweet and just misunderstood by the others. After the bugging incident, she wasn't so sure. When Marvin was around other people, she sensed hostility. And something else she couldn't identify. But it felt positive or at least earnest.

"You go on," Audrey told Lee. She would take care of Marvin.

Marvin followed Audrey to the buffet table, trying to convince her they should team up to find their contacts. Audrey was tempted but MOLECHECK had warned them other teams would be working against them. That was until she noticed Eric Little, leaning against the table, talking to Katy Diggs and Trevor James of Theta team.

"Could you do me a favor, Marvin?" Audrey nodded in the direction of Eric. "Would you please distract him for me?"

She gave Marvin a small shove toward Eric.

"Okay, but it's Ralph," Marvin said a little too loudly.

Audrey didn't care what his alias was. Eric was watching her, and she needed to get away. She cut through the new arrivals, past Lee, who still hadn't approached the Chairman, and ducked into a large reception room.

Audrey needed to find Curtis Klinovich. The faster she could get it over with the better. She glanced around the room. Everyone was already talking to someone. Audrey focused on the men. She went up to Instructor DASH first and introduced herself as Lena Rose, her alias for the exercise. DASH said he was Harold Pinot, an astronomer at the Ivanistan University. After a short conversation about stars in the southern hemisphere, Audrey excused herself. She lingered next to Tina Packard and Brooks Field of Epsilon who were talking to MOLECHECK. From their conversation, it was clear MOLECHECK was not a native of Ivanistan. Curtis Klinovich was born and raised in Ivanistan. Audrey moved on.

Finding Klinovich was harder than she expected. She decided a leathery faced man wearing a military uniform was definitely not her target. Klinovich was a photographer, not a soldier. She eliminated the Theta and Zeta homeroom instructors, who introduced themselves as musicians, before she was trapped by a man named Jonas who worked for the Ivanistan Daily News. He wanted to know what Audrey thought about Ivanistan cultural attractions. She escaped with a plea to use the restroom. Forty-five minutes were gone. She had 10 minutes left to find her contact.

She spotted Tex in the entryway talking with Mr. Brenjovic. He looked relaxed, like he was having fun. She was the one that should be enjoying this exercise. She leaned against one of the small entry tables waiting for their conversation to end. Minutes ticked by. She rose onto her toes and bounced a few times. She wrapped one leg around the other and did a small twist. Eric Little entered the room, busy adjusting a button on his jacket. Audrey sank to her knees, praying he had not seen her. Time was up; she needed to get to Tex.

She grabbed a cocktail napkin and pulled a pen from her purse. She scribbled: *I need your help now.* Then she folded the napkin several times until it fit in her palm. This was her chance to do a brush pass for real. She took a deep breath and headed straight for Tex.

"Excuse me." Audrey brushed against the back of Tex while slipping her note into his jacket pocket. She continued into the sunroom, forcing herself not to look back.

A few moments later, Tex sauntered into the sunroom. "Great brush pass, Aud." He held her folded napkin, which he wrapped around a scone, loaded with strawberry jelly and cream. "Problem is I can't read what you wrote."

"Never mind. You're here. I need your help," Audrey whispered.

"You look like the cheese fell off your cracker. Can't find your contact?"

"I've talked to all the instructors. He's probably left, if he was ever here." Audrey sighed. "How'd yours go?"

"Easy as falling of a log. He likes hiking. We're hitting the trails this weekend."

"Nice. I should be eliminated by then."

"Buck up, girl. You're doing great."

"Doing great? I almost got thrown out for cheating, and now I'm failing the one thing every girl should be good at."

"Listen to me," Tex whispered, putting down his half-eaten scone. "I saw the grading sheet yesterday. MOLECHECK left it in the classroom, I guess by accident, or maybe on purpose. Lee's the one in trouble. I saw a P next to his name."

Audrey's thoughts jumped to p's she associated with Lee: perceptive, principled, promising, pockets, partner, and patient, perspicacious, pleasant—

"It don't stand for perfect, if you get my drift."

Audrey wrinkled her nose. "P words are popular, see there's another one, but—"

"Probation," Tex interrupted. "You've probably don't know much about that; I'm an expert in this area. But the important thing is you can do this, you just got to believe in yourself. Now get back in the saddle."

Audrey returned to the dining room, feeling a tiny bit more confident after Tex's pep talk. Eric Little leaned against the arched doorway, smiling at her. Her stomach dropped. He was the only one she had avoided talking to, and now he was coming toward her.

"Hello. I don't think we've met."

"Yes. No. I mean we don't have to meet."

"I'm Curtis Klinovich." He held out his hand.

NO. They could not do this to her. HE COULDN'T BE. "Mr. Klinovich—" Audrey stepped back.

"Call me Curtis. And you are?" His hand was still outstretched.

Eric smiled, his eyes cold. Audrey's mind went blank. She couldn't for the life of her remember her alias.

"Curtis, yes. Well, um. How do you know the Brenjovic's?" Her mind was racing. She needed to concentrate, to get a feel for what game he was playing.

"They sponsored my last show."

"Show?" The room became unbearably hot. A trickle of sweat slid down the small of her back. She searched the room looking for someone who might save her.

"Yes, I'm a photographer. And you are?"

"Oh, I'm not that interesting." Audrey spotted Lee and jerked her head several time to get his attention. But Lee turned away. You cowardly geek, Audrey wanted to scream. See if I help you in the future.

"I've told you about me, why don't you tell me a little about you," Eric asked, stepping closer.

Audrey tried to pull back but she was already wedged against the china cabinet. "What do you shoot?" she heard herself ask a little too loudly.

Eric smiled, flashing his white teeth. "Birds of prey. Did you know that once their talons dig into an animal, their reflexes won't let them release until the animal stops moving?" Eric demonstrated the action of the talons in the pocket of air between them.

Audrey's head smacked hard against the cabinet doors. "It sounds so…." Audrey swallowed hard, a sick lump in her throat. She no longer felt hot, but freezing cold.

"Not interested in the wildlife?" Eric turned to leave.

Audrey sensed his triumph at her failure. He had done this on purpose, to intimidate her. She fingered her necklace.

"No, I do. You make it sound so…so dramatic."

Eric, a.k.a. Curtis Klinovich, kept walking.

Audrey leapt forward, cutting him off. "But you're probably exaggerating."

"That sounds like a challenge." Eric's eyes narrowed.

"No. But I'd like to see for myself. Can I come along the next time you have a photo shoot?"

"Let's meet next Saturday, 6:00 a.m. You should tell me your name first…"

— • — • • • — • • • — — — • — — — — — • •

Memo for the Record
Date/Time: 6 JUL/2215Z
To: CONTROL
Info: MOLECHECK
From: BULLDOG
Re: Operation Tea Party — Recruit MIND-READER

MIND-READER got off to a timid start, waiting for me to approach her at the end of the party. She collected a minimum of background information and set up a follow-up meeting, but only after I pushed her. She has an annoying habit of staring without saying a word. It would make a normal person feel self-conscious and exposed.

Assessment: She must be more aggressive. Spies cannot be timid. Grade: Fair

Crash, Bang, Zoom

Spy training moved into the fifth week, and Tex no longer complained about being bored. Each day was packed with agent meetings, learning to break into rooms without leaving behind any sign of secret searches, and writing and breaking codes. He looked forward to every day and each new challenge. The marks from his instructors were good, sometimes great. Not like at school, where the teachers wrote him off as not knowing a widget from a whangdoodle. Tex knew that if he could make it through the next training segment, he'd be the Bond of all Bonds. When—not if, Tex told himself, setting his jaw.

"ATTEN-TION!" A wiry man paced the parking lot in front of Tex and the recruits from Alpha, Kappa and Zeta teams, eying each one of them. His skin was the color of sunbaked leather, tough and crinkled like an alligator's back. Dressed in head-to-toe camouflage fatigues that blended in with the trees, he would almost disappear in a blink before suddenly reappearing while he reviewed his troops. He carried a clipboard tucked under his arm like a weapon to be drawn at a moment's notice. "My name is DUTCH. This is *my* training field. When you are on *my* training field, I *own* you. You do whatever I say. UNDERSTOOD?"

Ria's hand popped up. Without waiting to be recognized, she fired off her questions. "Why do you call it crash and bang? Will we be actually crashing cars? Like demolition derby? What does this have to do with spying? Does everybody…"

Tex groaned. What was it with her jawin'? Couldn't she shut up and let the man speak? His nerves were already on edge at the prospect of getting back behind the wheel. What if he couldn't do it? What if he froze in front of all of them? What if they laughed at him?

DUTCH moved in front of Ria. He stared her down like he was contemplating squashing a pesky fly. "I awhhhh—" Ria stopped mid-sentence when DUTCH's face came even with hers.

"I asked if you understood. I didn't ask for your idle thoughts. UNDERSTOOD?"

"But—"

"I CAN'T HEAR YOU."

"YES, SIR," she shouted, this time at the top of her lungs. Then she snapped her mouth shut. Tex marveled at DUTCH. How did he do it?

"THAT'S BETTER. Yesterday, I had problems with Sigma team not following the safety rules. When I say if you drive into a ditch, do not try to drive out on your own, but radio for help, I mean it. Sigma team now has two fewer recruits. UNDERSTOOD?"

"YES, SIR," the recruits responded. Tex glanced down the line of intimidated recruits; he suspected none of them knew how to drive, let alone how to get out of a ditch. He doubted anyone would be dumb enough to ask DUTCH further questions.

"This is a defensive driving class. I'm here to teach you the maneuvers you can make with your vehicle to get yourself out of threatening situations. You will learn high speed driving, in forward and reverse. You will learn how to back away from roadblocks by doing reverse 180s and how to ram 'em. This is training for emergency purposes and for Ivanistan only. The legal age for driving in Ivanistan is 13. I DO NOT want to hear about any of you trying these maneuvers with the family car. I REMIND YOU none of you are old enough to legally drive on the streets of America. UNDERSTOOD?"

"SIR, YES SIR," the recruits hollered. Lee looked to Tex and mouthed, "Ditch?"

"Gotta be careful you don't flip the car," Tex whispered back.

"YOU HAVE SOMETHING TO SHARE OVER THERE?" DUTCH hollered.

"SIR, no sir," Tex bellowed.

"What's your name, boy?"

"COW-BOY, sir."

DUTCH looked down at the clipboard. "COW-BOY, I see here you've got some experience at high speed driving already. The Mogobi Grand Prix. Very good. I expect you to set an example for your team." DUTCH gave Tex a sharp salute, which Tex returned, the sick feeling in his stomach growing.

"SIR, QUESTION, SIR," Tex shouted.

"SPEAK."

"SIR, on the way here, we passed a shooting range. Since I'm an experienced driver, could I be reassigned to the range?"

"You did NOT see a shooting range. Recruits in Ivanistan are NOT issued firearms NOR trained on firearms. You WILL proceed with this training. UNDERSTOOD?"

"YES SIR, thank you SIR." Tex tried not to show he was nervous as a porcupine in a balloon factory. Trading the car for the range would have been too perfect. He didn't buy the denial. He knew a shooting range when he saw one. Tex saluted again.

DUTCH resumed his briefing. "The rest of you recruits will need to crawl before you can run. You will drive in teams, taking turns. Grab a suit and helmet and go to your cars."

Lee and Audrey were assigned a brown 1985 Oldsmobile 88 Royale and Leila Abbas and Ian Hawkins of Zeta a white one. Marvin and Hannah ended up with the newest car, a 1987 Dodge Diplomat. Tex didn't know which was worst: driving again or driving with Ria in the junker assigned to them. The 1982 Chrysler Fifth Avenue had smashed-in bumpers, dented doors and by the looks of the front grill, an abused engine. Compared to modern cars, it was huge with the street power of rear-wheel drive.

Tex sorted through the helmets and silver flame-resistant suits for a set his size. Hands shaking, he slipped into silver coveralls and pulled the long zipper in the front. "You go first," Tex told Ria without looking up.

"Sure. I've read how-to books on driving. It's a cinch," Ria said.

Tex turned and faced Ria. She stood erect, helmet tucked under her arm, posing like a racecar driver at the finish line. Except she had her suit on backwards.

"On second thought. I'll go first." Tex tried to keep his voice steady, but it came out an octave higher than usual. He slipped in behind the steering wheel. The helmet and suit brought back a flash of memories. Bad ones. Could Ria see his hand shake when he reached for the ignition? It had been a year since Tex had been at the wheel of a car. A year since his cousin and racing partner was killed. His hands, slick with sweat, tightened around the black plastic.

"Yeah, nobody can accuse us of scratching the paint," Ria said. She pushed random buttons on the dashboard while continuing to talk nonstop. Tex didn't think she'd come up for air. He ran his hands down the side panel, searching for a button to lower the window. Beads of sweat were running down his face. How did he open the blasted window? He hit the glass with his palm. Ria stopped messing with the radio and looked at him. "You okay?"

"I need some air." Tex hit the window again. Maybe the entire pane would fall out of the rusted frame.

"You turn the handle." Ria hit the radio buttons again.

"Do wut?"

"You gotta turn it." Ria wiggled the handle on her side of the. Tex cranked the handle and stuck his head out the window. Around him car engines revved, and horns honked. He needed to pull it together.

"Well, are you going? Everyone's waiting on you."

Tex looked over to see Ria watching him. He glared at her and hit the gas, bracing himself against the steering wheel. The engine roared, but the car did not move. DUTCH's voice bellowed through the radio. "COW-BOY, stop gunnin' the engine. That baby's gotta last you through three weeks of training. You blow the engine; you put in a new one. UNDERSTOOD?"

Ria stared at Tex. "What's the matter? Are you nervous? It's okay because—"

"NO TALKING!" Tex yelled, trying to sound like DUTCH.

Ria turned away, her hair springing in all directions. She slumped deeper into the passenger seat and fussed with her bracelet making it clatter in the most annoying way.

Tex grabbed the gearshift, pulling the shaft toward D for drive. He felt his heart pounding. He placed his foot on the gas pedal. The car lurched forward. The pounding didn't stop. Pain seared his brain with each throb. What if something went wrong again? Why'd Ria have to be in the car with him? It was his fault his cousin was dead because they had argued, like with Ria. He remembered yelling at his cousin as the car clipped the barrier and flipped, rolling down the cliff. Tex was thrown clear of the car and blacked out. It was the last time Tex saw his cousin. The gas tank exploded, incinerating the car and everything in it. His cousin's body was never recovered.

Tex raced down the marked course in a blur, screeching through the orange cones. He pulled to a quick stop and fled from the driver's seat. "Just like in the books. Right?"

Trading places with Ria was agony. She couldn't get a feel for the brakes. She hit them hard, sending Tex lurching toward the windshield, saved only by his seat belt.

"Watch it" Tex said. "You trying to kill us?"

Ria didn't say a word. She didn't need to. Tex was surprised she could irritate him in complete silence.

The radio crackled. DUTCH told them to move on to road navigation. He instructed them to take the route designated on the clipboard in the car. It was a timed exercise to practice determining direction and making quick turns.

"Remember, radio if you get stuck," DUTCH said.

"I'll go first." Tex grabbed the clipboard. After switching places with Ria, he spun the Chrysler out on the paved road before Ria could fully click her seatbelt into place. The sooner he finished the course, the sooner he could get away from Ria and the car.

Ria leaned across to grab the clipboard.

"I can read it myself." Tex placed the clipboard in his lap and made the second turn so sharp Ria clutched her stomach and turned a bit green. Tex ignored her. He wanted out. He had done the cones. He could drive on the road. Kiddie stuff, he told himself. No reason to chew his bit.

Tex followed the directions on the clipboard, cutting through the woods on narrow lanes, and crisscrossing the camp. He drove in silence, listening to the music, ignoring the occasional glare from Ria when he took a corner particularly fast.

Every so often recruits passed them, heading the opposite direction. Only then did Tex slow, not trusting these newbie drivers to be able to judge the width of the road. He had no intention of ending up in a ditch and calling DUTCH for help.

Tex was halfway finished with his course when he drove out of the woods into an open meadowland. On the far side, he saw a car in a ditch. Marvin and Hannah's. He wouldn't have looked twice if he hadn't noticed Marvin was not in the car, but running fast as greased lightning across the meadow away from them and toward the tree line. The silver suit made him stand out against the green background. Suddenly, Marvin dropped and hid in the tall grass. Tex figured Marvin had noticed their car.

"Hey, look over there." Ria pointed toward the stopped car. "That's Hannah. We should go help her."

"There's no road over there." Tex kept to the lane, which turned back into the woods. Once screened by the trees, Tex stopped. Sure enough, after a few seconds, Marvin popped out and ran towards the far trees. Marvin was up to something. Tex was determined to find out what it was. He unfolded a large map of the campgrounds.

"Are you going back to help?" Ria said in surprise.

"No. I'm double-checking the route."

"What if you needed help? You'd want someone to stop." Ria wasn't giving up.

"DUTCH said to radio him. Not me." Tex applied the gas. Rather than staying on the paved lane, he turned off onto a dirt track. According to the map, the track cut back along the outer fence line in the direction Marvin was heading. The road was narrow and pitted with boulders. The old Chrysler bounced and shimmed.

Ria screamed at Tex to slow down. "Where are you going?"

Tex ignored her. He continued to track Marvin's movement through the trees. He was definitely heading for the outer fence. But why?

The track turned again and headed back toward the meadow. Tex pulled off to the side and stopped. He didn't want to get out in the open where Marvin could see him. He put the car in park, pulled off his helmet and unzipped his suit. "I gotta see a man about a dog," Tex said.

"Huh?" Ria said, shaking her head in confusion.

Tex laughed. Miss know-it-all didn't speak Texan. "I'll be back. Nature calls." Tex stepped out of the coveralls and headed in Marvin's direction.

"Boys." Ria sounded disgusted, but Tex doubted she'd follow him. He didn't want her to know he was tracking Marvin. They were teammates, and she'd tell.

Tex was certain he could nail Marvin this time. When Marvin stopped and looked back, Tex stopped and stayed with the trees, knowing his dark colored shirt and pants would blend in with the shadows. Sure enough, Marvin stopped when he reached the fence. He unzipped his driving suit, pulled something out and chucked it over the fence. He looked around again before running back in the direction of Hannah and their car.

Tex waited for Marvin to disappear into the woods. Using the hunting skills he learned from his pa, he crept over to the fence. On the other side, outside the campground, was a dirt road, wider than the track on which he left the Chrysler, and a large metal trash bin, the kind trash trucks pick up with mechanical arms. And nothing else but the sound of birds and crickets.

What did Marvin toss? Tex scanned the ground between the fence and the trash bin. There were leaves, pinecones, rocks, and sticks, nothing that didn't belong there. Something scurried across the track and disappeared around the base of the trash bin. Tex saw enough of the tail, long and thin, to know it was a rat. He resumed his study of the ground and saw a second rat, sitting still in the short grass.

A horn blared. Startled, Tex almost touched the electric fence. He'd forgotten about Ria. Something got her tail up. With one more sweep of the area, Tex headed back, no wiser than he had been 10 minutes before. That weasel got away again.

When Tex got back, he was surprised to find Ria not in the car, but sitting on a rock in the sun, her helmet off.

"Now's not the time for sunbathing. Let's go." Tex felt better chewing out Ria.

"I don't think we're going anywhere," Ria said.

"Why not?" Tex said.

Ria pointed at the car. The rear wheels had sunk down into mud. "You can radio DUTCH and explain why we're stuck in the woods by the instructors' houses and not on the road on the other side of camp, like your instructions say we're supposed to be."

Tex groaned. How would he ever live this down? He walked around the car. There had to be a way to get it out without calling DUTCH. Tex had been stuck in the sand a couple times during the Mogobi Grand Prix and used boards and chains to free the wheels. Maybe the same technique would work in mud.

"We can get out by ourselves. You need to do exactly what I say when I say. No questions. UNDERSTOOD."

"You're the one who doesn't understand anything, buster. I don't take orders from anyone, especially boys." Ria turned her back on Tex.

Tex groaned. "Ria! If we don't finish on time, they'll laugh at me 'cause they know I can do this with my eyes closed, but you, maybe you'll get eliminated."

If looks could kill, Tex figured he'd be dead meat. Ria turned and stared him down like she expected him to sink into the mud.

"The longer we wait, the deeper the wheels are gonna sink."

"Call DUTCH." Ria crossed her arms.

"I promise not to order you around. I'll say please." Tex was begging now.

Slowly Ria uncurled from her rock. "You owe me and don't forget it." Together they collected pinecones and sticks. Tex packed the pinecones into the mud in front of and behind the rear tires. Then he wedged in the sticks.

"You get behind the wheel and step on the gas when I say," Tex told Ria. He repeated the sentence twice with extra pleases before she moved. Tex stood behind the car, crouched slightly, his back against the bumper. "Hit it. Please." The engine gunned. Tex pushed up and back. The wheels spun. The car inched forward, then dropped back down into the divot, digging in deeper. "STOP." Tex smacked the trunk lid with this fist.

Nothing was going right. What kind of a spy was he if he couldn't handle the unexpected? Tex repeated his efforts, gathering twice as many pine cones and sticks. The car looked like it was sitting on a beaver dam by the time he finished.

"This time hit the gas harder when you start." Tex quickly added a "Please."

Tex smacked the trunk, signaling Ria to start. The engine gunned. Tex heaved. The car jolted. Pinecones flew. Mud splattered Tex's legs. The rear of the car fishtailed and then lurched forward. Tex fell hard, face first. Ria continued driving down the path, leaving him in the mud. He jumped to his feet and dashed after the car. "STOP!"

Ria sped up.

"PLEASE?"

Ria didn't stop, but screamed out the window. "Why? You don't help anyone else. News flash. You're no James Bond." Ria hit the gas. With her hand waving out the window, the charm bracelet clinking in the wind, Ria left Tex in the dust.

— • — • • • — • • • — — • — — — — • •

Memo for the Record
Date/Time: 20 JUL/1830Z
To: CONTROL
From: Security
Re: Operation Crash and Bang

Two cars have been observed entering an unauthorized area during Crash and Bang. Vehicle #5, assigned to COW-BOY and PUZZLE-GIRL, and vehicle #7 assigned to EAGLE-EYES and NIGHT-WIND. #7 was parked on the side of the road for several minutes. Vehicle #5 was unaccounted for 30 minutes.

Security sent a patrol to investigate and found COW-BOY outside of his vehicle. COW-BOY dissembled when asked where his car was, claiming a stomach ailment. The patrol turned him over to Instructor DUTCH.

MOLE Trail

Tex filled in Audrey and Lee on his Marvin sighting in homeroom that afternoon. His story about seeing Marvin throw something over the fence confirmed Lee's suspicion that Marvin was up to no good. Audrey defended Marvin, insisting he was misunderstood. She claimed she had sensed his inner chi, and it was not evil.

"I don't know about his insides, but outside, he's a complete snake," Tex said. "I just can't catch him red-handed."

"Did Ria see him too? Lee asked. "A witness might be useful."

Tex looked down, suddenly busy with his spy manual. "Nah, we got separated."

"I was wondering why Ria was at lunch, and you weren't," Audrey said.

Lee studied Tex. "How did you get sep—"

The appearance of MOLECHECK cut Lee short.

"I know you are all revved up from this morning, but it's still review time. We are starting the second half of the course, and it's only going to get harder from now on," MOLECHECK said. "So, listen up."

Lee's stomach tightened. Maybe that extra helping at lunch hadn't been such a good idea.

"By now you probably realize that being a spy is nothing like the movies." MOLECHECK took a seat at the head of the table, dropping the reports in front of them. "Unlike Hollywood's version of spies, you get graded. If you don't make the grade, you'll be eliminated."

"I don't think this is going to be a pep-talk on how great we are doing," Lee whispered to Audrey as he sank lower in his chair.

"I have the instructor reviews from your first agent meeting at the tea party. I'll meet privately with each of you, but there are some comments I want you all to hear. We don't expect perfect performances, but we do expect you to learn from your mistakes."

The room grew still. Lee clutched at his stomach hoping to stop a growl.

"We had some pathetic performances, including one recruit who gave up and sat in the corner eating."

Lee took a sharp breath and felt Audrey's eyes on him. She'd seen him chowing down at the buffet table instead of talking with the Minister.

"Another recruit failed to meet her assigned contact and instead cornered someone else's."

Audrey twitched in her seat.

"What else?" MOLECHECK flipped through his notes. "A conversation is a give-and-take between two or more people. If you want information, you should not drill the person with question after question. A conversation is not an interrogation."

"That's got to be PUZZLE-GIRL." Tex laughed. "A contact would probably agree to do anything just to get her to stop jawin'. That girl's got a 10-gallon mouth."

"Elicitation is the art of getting someone to talk about himself. Start by telling them something about you, like where you are from, and then let them respond. This is how we start friendships." MOLECHECK paused for a moment. "Although insulting a contact is normally not a good way to build rapport. LAB-MAN, I mean you."

A bead of sweat dripped down Lee's forehead onto his glasses.

"While I realize foods from other countries are new to most of you, spitting out a half-chewed salt cheese is considered rude. Try holding it in a napkin until you can dispose of it."

"COW-BOY." MOLECHECK checked his clipboard. "A word of warning. Get your facts straight on Ivanistan. You can't bluff your way through everything."

"Yes, Sir!" Tex responded with a grin and a triple rotation in his chair.

Lee liked Tex, but it bugged him that nothing seemed to get to the guy. He never seemed stressed or sweaty, or out of control.

"Your write-ups on the meeting were poor to terrible." MOLECHECK waved the reports in the air. "Every report must include the basic information of who, what, when, where and why. In half of them, I couldn't tell the difference between the raw intelligence and the assessment. If your contact tells you he is an ax murderer that is raw intelligence. If you find a bunch of chopped-up bodies in the safe house, and you think he did it, you are making an assessment. I want the reports redone and back to me by 8:00 tonight."

"Yeah, I'd be assessing not to meet that dude in any safe house." Tex grinned.

"But did we pass?" Audrey's voice was a mere gasp under the tightly wrapped chain.

"All of you managed to do the minimum. While that got you through to the next round, next time it won't."

How did Audrey skate through without being picked on by MOLECHECK, Lee wondered? Was she that good?

"I'm passing out information to help you prepare for your next meeting. Read it carefully and begin writing an ops-planning report. Tomorrow morning we start another technical component on dead drops." MOLECHECK slid a folder from the pile in front of each one of them. "Also, we are missing some concealment devices from DASH's lab. The dead rat and the soda can. If you have them, please return 'em."

Tex sat up straight and struck his palm against his forehead.

"Something to say, COW-BOY?" MOLECHECK asked.

"No, sir. Just remembered something."

MOLECHECK's serious face disappeared and the twinkle returned to his eyes. "I understand our mysterious prankster has struck again. Our female campers might want to check the watchtower to see if they are missing any unmentionables."

Audrey's face went beet red. "Like what?"

"I noticed a couple of extra items flapping from the flag pole. I'm sure CONTROL will have something to say about it, but I think you guys have a mole problem."

"A mole?" Tex asked.

"Yes, someone who is working against you from the inside. Sounds like a counterintelligence problem to me. Now get to work."

MOLECHECK had barely left the room, when Lee pulled out the extra fortune cookies he pocketed from lunch. He was not in the mood to read all the red marks smeared across his contact report. He glared at the B-. Good thing his mother would never see this. A- was the Asian F.

"I knew it." Tex leaned across the ops table to snatch a cookie. "EAGLE-EYES put down a dead drop. I saw two rats. One was alive. The other didn't move. I bet you it was the missing rat. That boy is as crooked as a dog's hind leg. The question is what is he up to?"

"Trouble," Lee said. He told them about the day in the Commo Lab when Marvin wrote something in invisible ink and then folded it very carefully, like he planned to use it later. "It seemed odd at the time, but maybe it was the message he passed this morning."

"Did either of you notice the flag pole? I'd die if…do you think EAGLE-EYES is the one doing the pranks?" Audrey snatched a cookie from Lee's pile.

"Hey, get your own," he protested.

"You can have the cookie. I need the fortune." Audrey split the cookie in half and pulled out a slip of white paper. Her face brightened. "It's my lucky numbers! I know it's a sign!"

Lee shook his head. "They're probably all the same. Seriously, Marvin is a sly one if he stole the concealment device. That case was locked." Lee wanted to keep the focus on Marvin and the rat.

"Kids who do pranks are funny. I don't know about you, but Marvin doesn't make me want to laugh." Tex said. "I wouldn't trust him farther than I can throw him."

"I don't think he's all bad," Audrey said. "Did either of you notice the flag pole?"

"You're kidding me, right? Has he brainwashed you?" Lee wiped the sweat streak off his glasses with the front of his shirt.

"He made me something. It was thoughtful. Who would be able to climb—?"

"He made me something too. A coin with a bug in it," Lee said. "You saw what kind of trouble that got us into."

"There was never any proof Marvin made that coin. He said he found it and gave it to you because he was trying to make friends," Audrey said.

"Aud, not everyone is as nice as you are. Marvin is a schemer."

"Sitting here arguing about him won't do any good. We have to set a trap for him," Tex said.

"How?" Lee asked.

Tex tossed his fortune on the table in front of Lee. "You can't get lard unless you boil the hog." He barreled out of the homeroom.

Lee picked up the message. It read *Good Luck is the Result of Good Planning*. And the lucky numbers were different from Audrey's.

— • — • • • — • • — — • — — — — • •

Memo for the Record
Date/Time: 20 JUL/2230Z
To: All Homeroom Instructors
From: CONTROL
Re: Mid-Term Status Report

Alpha team: COW-BOY – Pass
                 MIND-READER – Pass
                 LAB-MAN – Pass, provisional

Kappa team: EAGLE-EYES – Pass
                 NIGHT-WIND – Pass
                 PUZZLE-GIRL – Pass

Omega team: MAP-FINDER – Pass
                 STEALTH-RIDER – Selected Out

Zeta/Epsilon FOX-GLOVE – Selected Out
teams   MATCH-MAKER – Pass, provisional
                 KEY-FINDER – Pass
                 GATE-KEEPER – Pass

Theta team: SAIL-FISH – Pass
                 PIX-STAR – Pass, provisional
                 TRAIL-LEADER – Pass

Sigma/Iota   TRUTH-DIGGER – Selected Out
teams   BEAD-WEAVER – Selected Out
                 DRAW-MASTER – Selected Out

Masquerade

Audrey walked through the summer crafts fair and farmer's market in a town a few miles from Camp International, feeling confident. She'd survived the tea party with Eric and was still in the competition. He gave her barely passing marks, dinging her for waiting so long to talk with him. *Spies can't be timid*, he wrote. Yes, but they can be jerks, Audrey almost told MOLECHECK before biting her lip. There were two weeks before the final exam. She'd show Eric and all the other instructors she wasn't timid.

She clutched at the blow-up tube wrapped around her waist, worried it would slip down over her narrow hips. She hoped VIOLET, their disguise instructor was right and people would only see a pleasantly plump woman with graying hair in a large print dress out for a bit of shopping, not a 13-year-old girl pretending Halloween had come early, or worse, a spy. Audrey tried her best to feel old, not just act old, adopting imaginary pains in her back, the kind her grandmamma used to complain about. VIOLET had taught them that their disguises should look natural, but completely change their appearance. And to pay attention to shoes; even the best covert operatives forget to change their shoes.

She wandered through a tent selling small metal sculptures shaped like people playing different sports. She pretended to admire the items for sale, but her real focus was on faces. There was a man with a bushy gray mustache who smiled at her. A mother in a sun hat held onto the hand of a small boy intent upon touching everything. A teenage boy with pimples wandered in a zigzag pattern. Was he with the skinny man with fuzzy brown hair wearing a baseball cap low over his eyes she had seen a few minutes earlier? Audrey tried to take a mental picture of each face. Distracted, she backed into the sharp corner of a table. Now her back really did hurt. Groaning, Audrey found acting old and keeping watch at the same time was backbreaking work.

She shuffled toward the next tent, setting up a random pattern to her movements. Normal people would visit the tents one after the other. If she used a mixed order, she'd be abnormal, and anyone following her would stand out. But then another thought occurred to her. What if they were normal abnormal people? How could she tell the difference?

The faces in the second tent were unfamiliar. A young couple holding hands. An old woman, stooped, and walking with a cane. A dark-eyed man with brown curly hair. A middle-aged woman with thick glasses and dull, straight hair. Audrey leaned in closer to get a sense of her.

The woman glared at Audrey and snatched a pink dog collar studded with rhinestones. "I saw it first. It's mine."

Startled, Audrey backed away and tried to act casual in front of a display of homemade dog treats. There was something oddly familiar about the woman.

Audrey passed by the next four tent rows and selected one on the opposite side of the square. She did not look over her shoulder or stop and re-tie her shoelaces. That's what amateurs do, according to MOLECHECK. She waited instead for an opportunity to step to one side to let a mother with a stroller pass and pretended to look at the baby. Her eyes scanned the scene behind her. There were many faces, but none looked familiar.

Audrey's heart quickened when she entered the farmer's market. Her agent, TINKER, had left a dead drop for her in this section. She had to stop herself from rushing to find the tent with fresh flowers. She couldn't be certain she wasn't being followed.

Instead Audrey entered a tent selling jars of homemade jelly and jam. A lady offered her a slice of bread smeared with blackberry jam. De-licious. Lee would like this tent. Audrey nibbled at the sweet treat, eyeing jam labels and faces. A man with a ball cap and a gold earring. A young woman in shorts. Was she with a guy before? Audrey wasn't sure. She stayed in the back of the tent, determined to wait the girl out. How long could a normal person look at jam without buying? Audrey kneeled down, like she was looking at the jars in a box on the floor. She wanted to see the girl's shoes. That way she'd recognize her if the girl crossed her path again.

The sun beat on the backside of the tent, casting shadows of people walking by. "Do roosters always crow at dawn?" she heard a familiar voice say.

"Yes, except if they have jet lag," a man responded, just above a whisper.

Audrey almost dropped the jar of blueberry jam. She looked at the shadows on the tent wall. One was shorter than the other. The voice sounded like Marvin.

Do roosters always crow at dawn? What an odd thing to say. It felt like a parole. *Yes, except if they have jet lag* had to be a counterparole.

They were speaking in whispers now, or had moved further away from the tent because Audrey couldn't make out what they were saying. Staring at the jam label, Audrey remembered VIOLET's instructions not to talk to anyone. Did Marvin have a different exercise? An agent meeting and not a dead drop assignment?

The shadows grew taller on the tent wall. They were coming closer. "...I can't get access to it," Marvin said. "I don't understand why you want me to do this."

"Keep trying. Now return this. It was stupid to take it."

The two shadows melded into one and then split, heading in opposite directions. Audrey set the jar down and hurried out of the tent. There was no sign of Marvin.

Anxious to get her mission done, she rushed toward the flower tent and nearly rammed into the back of a man wearing a cowboy hat. A weird feeling pulsed through her.

The tent was crowded with shoppers. None of the faces were familiar. Then they all seemed suspicious. Audrey reached for the necklace tucked under her blouse, then stopped. VIOLET warned against wearing identifying jewelry because it could give them away.

Audrey moved to the rear and looked for a crate holding clippers and gloves. It was shoved halfway under a table filled with vases of dahlias and coneflowers. Using her foot to move the crate, she saw the dead drop: a blue and brown glove. Audrey surveyed the faces once again. A thin man with a cowboy hat and a camera around his neck had his overly large nose in a vase of tulips. A young man in shorts and a tank top was buying a bouquet of roses. A woman held up a gardening book. Didn't she have a kid with her before? When the woman put down the book and left the tent, Audrey decided her mind was playing tricks on her.

In one swift motion, Audrey bent down and reached for the glove. She pulled it out of the crate as the flash of a camera lit the interior of the tent. Audrey twirled around, the glove still gripped in her hand.

"Gotcha," Eric Little said from behind the camera. He reached up and tipped his cowboy hat in her direction.

— • — • • • — • • • — — • — — — — — • •

Memo for the Record
Date/Time: 27 JUL/1847Z
To: CONTROL
From: DASH
Info: Security
Re: Missing Concealment Device

While conducting inventory of classified holdings I discovered two devices missing from their cases: the dead rat and the soda can concealment devices. I advised all homeroom instructors to ask their teams about the missing items, requesting they be returned. They have not been recovered. It seems we have a recruit who is a thief. Request Security conduct a full investigation.

Value of missing property: $2350.

Dead Reckoning

The recruits were told to be ready at 0500 hours. Lee shuffled onto the cold bus and rested his head against the window trying to catch a few extra Z's during the ride. After six weeks of training, he knew to expect the unexpected. In the beginning, he hated the feeling that he was caught in a maze about to walk into a trap at each turn. Now, rather than worry, he made contingency plans, bringing the power of science and technology with him.

The sun was starting its crawl over the hills, tinting them shades of pink, and Lee couldn't help but notice, even through heavy eyelids, how beautiful this part of the country was. The morning air was crisp and smelled like a combination of wet leaves and wood smoke. The bus shimmied along dirt roads for 30 minutes before it groaned to a stop. The doors opened, and DUTCH climbed aboard, thermos in hand. He was like a Komodo dragon tracking his prey. Lee looked outside for other signs of danger. All he could see were trees.

"Down to 13, I see." DUTCH took a sip of his coffee. "Wonder how many of you will be around for the bus ride back?"

Lee exchanged knowing looks with Audrey. Don't let them psych you out.

"This is a land navigation, escape and evasion exercise." DUTCH took another swig of coffee. "You will each start at a different location. You will follow your maps to locate and retrieve your navigation flags." He motioned to Eric Little and Devin Bassett, who boarded behind DUTCH. "These guys will be tracking you. If we find you before you find your way out with your three flags, you're out. UNDERSTOOD?"

Lee could tell this was going to be an awfully long day. Mostly awful.

He noticed Audrey kept her head down as she moved through the line towards Eric. When she reached for her map, Eric held tight, forcing her to look at him.

"I'll see you out there," he said.

Maybe Audrey was right that Eric had it in for her.

ATVs dropped recruits off in pairs at remote locations. Two small yellow flags marked the start positions for Ria and Lee. Ria grabbed her flag, with the number 6 written on it, and stuffed it in her backpack. Lee's was number 8. DUTCH told them they had to find and bring back the three yellow flags with their numbers on them to prove they could read and follow a map using only a compass and terrain features. Lee took a quick look at Ria's map; their next flags were in opposition directions. He was on his own.

He rotated his map until the north on his map lined up with north on his compass. A rocky ridge to his left was shown on the map by a series of curved lines; these contour markings indicated a change of height. The good news was he knew where he was. The bad news was where he had to go.

From his starting point, he needed to travel a mile southwest. The map contour markings showed he would be heading uphill most of the way. The next flag was in a low spot, a depression of some sort. One mile. And that was only the second flag. Lee figured Tex would be finished in an hour or less, while the rest of them were captured in the woods. The only way to raise his probability of lasting more than ten minutes was to stay off anything resembling a trail.

Fifteen minutes later, Lee regretted his decision. Off-roading, even on foot, was a lot tougher than he had calculated. He lost his first fight with a bramble bush, ripping his right cargo shorts pocket, his stash of M&Ms

and some flesh. He could grow new skin and live without the pocket. But no M&Ms? That was a crisis. Lee adjusted his backpack, which was growing heavy. He wished he had raided the kitchen instead of DASH's lab. The equipment he borrowed from the lab had better be worth its weight. Lee slowed his pace; crashing through underbrush would attract attention and invite more bramble attacks.

An hour later, Lee reached the top of a ridge and the overpowering smell of rotten eggs. He checked his armpits. It wasn't him. Peering down the other side, he saw a swampy pond that looked like it could be hiding some freaky bog monster, or at a minimum, snakes. The pond was in a clearing, a good place for an ambush. There was no avoiding it. According to the terrain markings on his map, his next flag was somewhere on the opposite side. Lee sighed. It could have been worse. The flag could be on top of the ridge to his right.

There was a crunch, and then something rustled behind him. Lee tensed. No way was he going to be dragged to the bottom of the murky waters by something with big teeth and stinky breath. He swung around, kicking out his left leg, like he'd seen his brothers do it in their Tae Kwon Do competitions. "HAH!" he yelled.

The monster recoiled and yelped. "AAH!"

Tex thudded against the rocky wall, fists up protecting his face, then straightened, trying to retain a bit of cool. "Scared ya," he said.

Lee fell to the ground laughing. He had scared the almighty Tex and himself. But Tex didn't let him enjoy his triumph. Instead he dropped down next to Lee and motioned to keep quiet. "Trackers," Tex mouthed. For a moment, Lee had forgotten about them. Tex's yell would have alerted even the most incompetent ones.

"Give me your map." Tex elbowed Lee.

"No, we're competing against each other."

"That's the thing. I'll be a skunk at a lawn party if our maps don't send us to the exact same spot."

"Why?" Lee said, a tight grip on his map.

"I didn't take off right away like everyone else. I dropped behind a tree and waited to see what moved."

"And?"

"I saw Eric Little and six other Trackers, not just Devin. They were pointing to their maps, saying how they'd use choke points to ambush us."

"Yeah, that's why I'm staying off the paths so I don't run into any check points."

"You don't get it. That's how my pa rounds up cattle. They'll use the terrain to herd us and ambush us in narrow points near our flags. The swamp looks like a trap to me."

"So we channel Audrey and do the unexpected?" Lee said.

"Exactly," Tex said. "We're going up." Tex pointed to the gray cliff, which went vertical for twenty feet.

Lee groaned.

Tex scrambled up the rock face with no hesitation while Lee struggled to find each foothold. His hands sweaty, he slipped several times, smacking his head into the rock.

"You're supposed to climb the rock, not sugar it." Tex grabbed Lee by the back of his shirt and pulled him the rest of the way.

Lee lay on his side looking out at the view. They were high above the tree line. From this vantage point, Lee could see the bog glistening in the sunlight and Brenton Meyers of Omega team and Tina Packard of Epsilon, poking the water with long sticks.

Tex lowered himself onto the rock next to Lee. He took binoculars out of his pack and scanned the pond and then the tree line. He pointed at something in the trees. Lee took the field glasses. Dressed in camouflage, the counselors moved slowly forward. Eric Little gave the signal. They burst out of the woods, trapping Brenton and Tina, yellow flags in their hands. Lee would have been nailed too if not for Tex.

"My flag is down there," Lee whispered.

"So is mine. We'll have to sneak in and grab them while the Trackers are ambushing someone else."

Movement caught Lee's attention. He watched Marvin stumble out of the trees near the bog and grab two yellow flags. He dashed toward the woods before the counselors could react. "Looks like Marvin has the same idea. But why two flags?"

"That weasel," Tex said. "He's stealing my flag. I'm gonna bust him like a ripe watermelon."

Tex started to get up, but Lee stopped him. "Wait. I have an idea. Keep your eye on Marvin." Lee took off his backpack and pulled out a netbook and a box the size of a briefcase. Snapping the locks open, Lee removed six metal pieces and started assembling them.

"What's that?"

"A drone. Watch for Marvin," Lee said. He unfolded two longer pieces and snapped them into place. Lee showed off the metal hawk.

"Well butter my biscuit. Where'd you get that?" Tex said.

"Kind of borrowed them from DASH's lab. I thought the field trip today might give me a chance to fly it." Lee connected the flight stick and powered up the computer. In less than five minutes the hawk drone was launched. It soared over the bog. Two video images appeared on the netbook screen, one a view through the hawk's eyes in the direction it was flying and the other of the view straight down. Lee made the hawk take several loops, getting the feel for the flight stick. It was like playing a video game.

"Now where's Marvin?" Lee asked once he was sure he could handle the bird.

"He's hiding behind the rock over there."

Tex pointed to an area just inside the tree line. From there Marvin would have a good view of the area where

Tex's flag used to be. "The worm is sticking around to watch what I'll do when I can't find my flag."

"Too bad hawks like worms." Lee put the bird into dive. "Watch this, worm!"

Marvin must have sensed something. He let out a screech as the hawk dove for his head. Marvin hit the dirt and rolled. The hawk dove at him again and again. Marvin kept scrambling until he splashed into the water. When he came up for air, he was covered in green swamp goop.

Tex covered his mouth with his forearm, to muffle his laughing and pointed to the camouflaged Trackers bounding toward Marvin.

Lee circled the hawk back toward the area where Marvin had been hiding. He swooped it down once again and hit the arrow key. "Darn, I missed." He made a second run. This time the hawk dipped down and then up, with two yellow flags caught in the claw feet. Lee brought the bird to a perfect landing on their rocky outcropping. "Which one is yours?" Lee asked, retrieving the flags.

"Number 7."

Lee took the flag and with a black pen wrote two zeros in front of the 7 before handing it to Tex.

Once Marvin's flag was back in the hawk's claws, Lee sent the bird flying. The counselors were still struggling in the water, trying to handcuff Marvin. He kept slipping away, only to be grabbed again. Lee took the bird toward Marvin, releasing its claw so the yellow flag splashed into the water behind the counselors. They turned and looked in the direction of the splash. The bird zoomed away.

"Why'd you do that? We should have kept it."

"Nah. Marvin's not going any further. He should have the flag as a souvenir of his life as a worm."

Lee took the drone back up. The bird's eye caught movement under the green slime about two feet away from Marvin and his captors. Eric Little, who had a hand on Marvin's shirt, suddenly screamed. He disappeared under the water. When he surfaced, he kicked and cursed at something in the boggy sludge. Marvin broke free, grabbed his flag and ran toward the woods. Lee circled the bird back for a second look. Eric kept turning like a top and pointing into the water. The other counselors had abandoned him for dry ground. Lee took the bird lower. The swamp monster was gone.

While Tex cursed at Marvin getting away, Lee zeroed the hawk on a yellow flag on the far side of the pond. The hawk swooped down. On the screen, Lee saw a black eight on the flag. He opened the claw of the bird. "Got it."

"Good going flying, ace. Let's get moving before we're spotted," Tex said.

After packing the flags and drone, they trekked along the ridge for another hour, before coming to a 30-foot drop. The only way across was a natural stone bridge. Lee took a deep breath, trying not to look down, and followed Tex across.

Shouts midway across drew his attention back to the swamp. Two recruits were fleeing toward the water as the counselors captured two other victims. Lee noticed none of the Trackers pursued recruits into the water.

"Better stay focused," Tex said. "They'll be looking for us next."

Lee was focused. His eyes were on a pair of turquoise sneakers barely visible behind a fallen log on the other side of the bridge. Creeping forward, he threw himself on the Tracker, intending to trap him under his weight. Except the Tracker was Audrey.

"Sorry." Lee rolled over into the soft leaves. "You okay?"

"I had a Tracker on my tail. I'm pretty sure it was Eric. I couldn't run anymore, so I decided to hide here until giant ants picked me up and carried me away."

"Or ate you." Lee said. Red splotches covered her face.

Audrey's hair was plastered to her head, and her shirt and jeans were wet and filthy, like she'd been crawling through green slime instead of walking. "Bugs are attracted to pale skin, there's nothing I can do about it."

"Whoa, you look like you've been chewed up, spit out and stepped on." Tex bent down to examine Audrey.

"You're both here!" Audrey squeaked.

"Keeping ahead of the Trackers. Have you found your second flag?" Tex said.

"How do you think I got this dirty?"

Lee looked at the green tinge to Audrey's hair. "Did you…"

"Swam the entire swamp." Audrey nodded. "They never saw me. I cut a reed so I could breathe without breaking the surface." Audrey beamed, giving off a greenish glow. So Audrey was the swamp monster. Eric Little was lucky to be alive.

"Are you sure you're not from Texas?" Tex gave Audrey a longhorn salute. Middle fingers down, forefinger and pinky raised. "Now give me your map." Tex spread out the three maps. "The last flags are all close. But look at the contour lines, four lines, and a 40-foot drop. They want to herd us down into a ravine so we have no way to escape."

"Not if we become birds," Lee said, grinning.

"Oooooh, we're going to fly?" Audrey charged off, arms flapping.

— • — • • • — • • • — — • — — — — • •

Memo for the Record
Date/Time: 30 JUL/2230Z
To: Security
From: CONTROL
Re: Operation Clean Up

Please remove from Bunkhouse One and Two the personal belongings of the following recruits now eliminated from the training program: Brenton Meyers, Omega; Tina Packard, Epsilon; Brooks Field, Epsilon; Laila Abbas, Zeta.

⑱
Hunting Season

Audrey's glee in escaping Eric's trap during the land navigation exercise evaporated a few days later when MOLECHECK told Alpha team their next assignment would test their ability to recruit agents. Hours of classroom time had been devoted to discussing the theory of agent development and agent acquisition, steps two and three of the Agent Recruitment Cycle. MOLECHECK said they were to assume for training purposes they had spent the past months developing a relationship with their contacts. Audrey's contact had been assigned the codename STRIKER and in the process of developing him she had learned that he had access to influential people inside the

Ivanistan labor unions. MOLECHECK instructed Audrey that intelligence on what the labor unions were doing was important, and she needed to recruit STRIKER.

This meant Audrey had to go head-to-head again with Eric, a.k.a Curtis Klinovich, wildlife photographer, a.k.a STRIKER. While she was happy she didn't have to spend months developing a friendship with him, Audrey was determined to be as bold and as aggressive as Eric had been with her at the tea party.

However, after an hour following Eric through the woods in search of wildlife, Audrey discovered his determination to intimidate her was far greater. Everything he said to her was an order or a criticism, like "Hurry up" or "Can't you be quieter?" Audrey kept apologizing. Everything he did showed he was in control, not Audrey.

"Don't move," Eric warned.

Audrey froze mid-step. His camera was pointed in her direction, at something over her left shoulder. She heard the camera click several more times in rapid succession and then a squawk and a flutter. She turned as a hawk rose from the meadow grasses.

"She missed it. Too bad," Eric said.

"Whaat?"

"Don't know. I didn't see it, but the hawk did." Eric studied the LCD display on his digital camera. "Beautiful creatures. Red-tailed hawks. Come, take a look."

Audrey walked over, worried that he had something up his sleeve.

The camera captured the hawk at the exact moment she was rising, wings spread, the long grasses draped from her talons. The colors were a blur of blues, browns, reds and greens.

"Wow, that's fantastic! You're a really good photographer." This was the first thing Audrey had said during the past hour that she meant.

"Do you really think so?" Eric asked. He sounded earnest for a change.

"Yes, you could probably sell it to National Geographic."

"I wish. My dream is to work for them as an international photographer. They would never hire me though."

"Why not?" Audrey asked.

"How would I ever get their attention living in Ivanistan?" Eric said, reminding her that he was Curtis Klinovich, amateur photographer in the pretend land of Ivanistan.

"You should send a sample of your work."

"I did, but no one responded."

MOLECHECK's words swirled in Audrey's brain. Successful agent recruitment is built on trust. You have to make the target trust you. One way is to help the target get something he otherwise cannot.

"Maybe I can help you. The father of a friend of mine works there." A pretend friend, Audrey reminded herself.

"Really? I could use an inside contact."

"I'll try. If your other photos are all this good, I'm sure they would be interested."

Audrey tried to relax. She took a seat under a tree. Maybe he wasn't as creepy as he seemed. She reached into her backpack and pulled out two paper bags. Her compact fell out with them. She removed two cans of soda from one bag. The other held six chocolate chip cookies, freshly made from the mess hall. Lee had given her the idea. She held out the bag to Eric.

"Thanks." He took four cookies.

Audrey held back an urge to tell him he was being greedy. Look for your target's vulnerability; something in his personality you can use to convince him that spying for you is in his best interest.

She snapped the compact open and closed absently, thinking about the scenario of Ivanistan, a country on the verge of war. "It's too bad you won't be able to come here for much longer."

"What do you mean?" Eric asked.

"If a war breaks out, this area will be too dangerous. The animals will leave, with all the bombing and fighting." Audrey tried to keep her voice casual. She didn't dare hope he would follow her lead.

"Why do you think there will be a war?" he asked.

"You've heard the rumors about groups trying to overthrow the government. If it happens, everyone says there will be war." Audrey angled the mirror of her compact to see how he was responding to her argument. He was sitting, head cocked in her direction, clearly interested.

"So you think a coup would be bad for the country?" he asked.

Make it personal. Make the target feel he has something to lose or to gain. "Yes. You wouldn't be able to do your photography. Living in town would be dangerous, too."

"But I've been told if the government was replaced, I'd be able to get a job."

"Sure, a job as a soldier or as a weapons dealer." The words slipped out an instant before she knew she had made a mistake. *Make the target believe there is a clear choice between something good for him or bad for him.* Eric would probably like being a soldier so he could kill things.

Eric grabbed his camera, snapping pictures of a tarantula-sized spider spinning a web in the foliage. Audrey dropped the compact and scooted away from the web. She waited for Eric to say something. The spider moved swiftly, knitting its web.

Eric cleared his throat.

The words came out of her mouth before her brain started working.

"You know, you could save these woods from the spiders."

"What?" Eric asked.

"I mean from the war." Audrey flushed. This was the moment. She had to ask. Her stomach was tied in knots. Her throat was dry. She thought about what MOLECHECK taught them—make the contact want to help. She took a deep breath then tucked a loose strand of hair behind her ear. She looked Eric straight in his too-blue eyes. *Make it personal. Put the benefits up front.*

"If there was no war, you would have the freedom to shoot all the wildlife pictures you wanted. You could become a famous photographer."

Eric laughed at her. "How am I going to stop a war?"

Audrey clutched her compact. "You told me you have a cousin in an important position in the labor union."

"Cousin Frederick? That jerk. What about him?"

"Could you introduce me to him? So I could explain how the opposition is lying to the labor unions. They want to get Ivanistan into the war, not help the people—"

"Why are you so interested? I mean, who are you working for?"

His eyes pierced into her, making the uncertainty flood back. "Well, I am…you see, the U.S. is worried about the people of Ivanistan. A war would be terrible and…well…we want to make sure it doesn't happen."

"Are you a spy or something?" Eric demanded.

155

"No," Audrey said, pulling back.

The sound of whistling and then footsteps echoed along the trail. Someone was coming.

"You're trying to get me in trouble. I'm going to the police." Eric sprang up and headed toward the sound.

"No wait." Audrey struggled to her feet, her compact flying to the ground. She ran forward and grabbed Eric's arm. "Do you care about your country or not?"

"Hey Odd," Jennifer said. "Whatcha doing?" She looked at Eric and raised her eyebrows suggestively. Two girls from Delta team raised their eyebrows too.

"Nature watching." Audrey released Eric's arm. She knew her voice came out a little too high.

"Not just watching, I'd say. You go girl," Jennifer added. "He's a cutie."

Audrey wished she could will the ground to open up and swallow her. Eric was walking away. If she didn't close the deal, he would rat her out as a spy.

"Wait!" Audrey shouted. Eric turned and so did Jennifer and her girls. "You forgot this." Audrey held Eric's tripod. She needed to get control of the situation. Jennifer and her friends continued down the trail, and Eric returned for the tripod. But Audrey wouldn't let it go. "I'm trying to help you."

"What makes you think I need help? I don't want to get mixed up with criminals."

"I don't want to get mixed up with criminals either. That's why I was so happy to meet you. I mean you're a good person who cares about things, like this forest."

Eric didn't say anything, but he stopped trying to leave. Audrey brushed the cookie crumbs off her fingers. She was going to do this if it killed her. The sounds of birds singing and bees buzzing made the moment feel less awkward. She no longer felt afraid. She was there to save him and the forest. She was on his side. He had to know that. She met his gaze, not as a challenge, but as an invitation to be her friend and partner.

"I work for people who care about Ivanistan and you. You can call me a spy, but that doesn't change anything. I want to help you. But I need you to help me. Will you introduce me to your cousin?"

— • — • • • — • • • — — • — — — — • •

Memo for the Record
Date/Time: 6 AUG/1700Z
To: CONTROL
From: MOLECHECK
Re: Alpha team Assessment

Recruit LAB-MAN overcame a number of challenges during the agent meeting. He handled the agent mix-up over the meeting location by insisting it was not the agent's fault. Recruit was less confident during the debriefing, losing control over the conversation. Overall, recruit needs to be more skillful in his questioning. Rather than playing upon friendship and trust, he went straight to the pitch. Because LAB-MAN's strengths are in the scientific field, special consideration should be given for his lack of strong interpersonal skills. Pass, provisional

Recruit COW-BOY handled the recruitment challenge with ease. He reviewed security and meeting arrangements after his agent went to the incorrect site. He manipulated the conversation to play upon trust and duty so that when he did give the pitch, the agent was ready to say yes. COW-BOY continued to mix up Ivanistan facts, showing lack of attention to detail and a cocky attitude on role-playing. Pass.

Recruit MIND-READER learned from past mistakes. She was more aggressive and took control over the course of the meeting. However, the instructor expressed concern about the randomness of her style and her disconcerting behavior, which made him "uncomfortable." When asked to describe the behavior, the instructor said MIND-READER made eye contact with him for prolonged periods like she was "staring deep in his soul." Pass, provisional.

The Diddle

MOLECHECK looked positively giddy the next morning. He wore a red tie with yellow smiley faces. "Don't get comfortable. You've all made the cut, and it's time for a field trip."

Audrey closed her eyes. She wouldn't have believed it if MOLECHECK hadn't said it out loud. The past few days with the late nights and heavy workload made her doubt her ability to read others' intentions. Last night at dinner, she had been talking to Hannah and felt a cold wind wash over her. The air smelled like burnt rubber or something even more toxic. Audrey knew at that moment her senses must be mixed-up if she thought Hannah was plotting against her.

"We'll be leaving in an hour for Washington, D.C. for your final exercise. You've survived seven weeks of rigorous training, and I know you all will make me proud."

Tex let out a loud hoot and spun around in his chair. Lee sat stunned.

MOLECHECK handed back their reports. "When we arrive, familiarize yourself with your operational environment. It might look like Washington D.C., but for this exercise it is Ivanistan. Don't be fooled by how normal it looks. Ivanistan is in crisis. Select sites to meet your agents. You must use your agents to figure out what is happening and decide what actions to take to protect American interests. You will also need to avoid the Ivanistan police. The FBI will be playing the role of the police, and let me warn you, they are very good. Be extra careful when you do your countersurveillance checks so that you do not bring the FBI along to your agent meetings. Unless you want to be arrested."

Audrey squeaked. The memory of getting caught unloading TINKER's dead drop was still fresh. She had never been arrested, and she was pretty sure she didn't want to be.

MOLECHECK held up a push-to-talk radio. "You'll need to take a bug-out kit. Be sure to pack a secure radio from the supply closet. You will only be able to communicate with your team. None of the other teams will be on your network. Your conversations will be monitored at all times by the senior staff, so if you don't want to be heard, say in the bathroom, remember to turn any electronics to off/standby. You each have been issued a secure netbook for writing your reports. Get your disguises, photo equipment and pack clothes for three days. Everything must fit in one pack."

Audrey was the last one to make it to the bus, laboring under the weight of her pack. A large silver bus that said Prescott Tours—See the real D.C. was waiting. MOLECHECK gathered the eight remaining recruits and announced they would be divided into two new teams.

"I can't believe Marvin's still here," Tex whispered to Audrey. "He's slicker than snot. How could MOLECHECK and CONTROL be so blind? They're supposed to be spies. Good ones."

"Listen up." MOLECHECK's eyes danced. Audrey sensed his smiley face tie was an inside joke.

"Kappa team, you'll split up. Marvin and Hannah, you'll join Katy and Trevor on Theta. Ria, you'll join Alpha."

Tex shot a pained look over at Audrey. It didn't take Audrey's special senses to see he didn't share MOLECHECK's enthusiasm about having Ria on their team.

"One last thing," MOLECHECK said. "I expect all of you to be on your best behavior outside the camp. CONTROL asked me to tell you that practical jokes will not be tolerated during the final exercise." Audrey blushed as she remembered her bra flapping at the top of the watchtower. "Someone turned a section of the lake into a bubble bath. With the waterfall churning, there's about eight feet of foam. And the place smells like strawberries."

MOLECHECK looked at Audrey, eyes twinkling, one eyebrow raised. "Come to think about it, you smell like strawberries."

Audrey followed Tex on to the bus, denying loudly that she was responsible for all the strawberries in the world. She used strawberry shampoo, but that didn't mean she was the practical joker. She was the victim, and she wanted everyone to know it.

Tex charged ahead to lay claim to the backbench. Audrey settled into a two-person seat in front of Tex, and six rows behind Marvin's team. No one wanted the front. The assistants were sitting there, including Eric Little. Audrey was starting to have mixed feeling about Eric, but wanted to avoid him as much as possible.

"I need your radios," Lee said as the bus made the first turn past the gate. "I worked out how to modify them for our own private frequency. No instructors, no other recruits listening."

Tex handed over his radio and reached over the seat for Audrey and Ria's.

"Why should I give it to you?" Ria asked, her voice hard as nails.

"Girl, you'd argue with a piece of wood," Tex said.

Neither Audrey nor Ria made a move to hand over their radios.

Tex waved his hand. "Give."

"I can't," Audrey wailed. They'd make fun of how much she packed and her certainty that she needed each item.

"Why not?"

"The zipper's stuck."

"Give it to me, I'll fix it."

"No, you'll break it."

"Give it." Tex reached over and wrestled the pack out of Audrey's arms.

"Fighting isn't going to help us." Lee grabbed at the pack as Tex wrenched it open. A curling iron, flat iron, hair dryer and three tubes of toothpaste fell at his feet.

"What's all this stuff?" Lee bent to pick up items from the floor. He held on to a tube of toothpaste figuring it might come in handy for one of his other inventions.

"Never mind." Audrey, who was now beet-red, squeezed past Ria and dropped to the floor. She shoved her belongings into her bag as fast as she could, crushing her wigs. She worked the zipper. Sure enough, it was broken. She knew she had overpacked, but in her rush to go, she knocked her hair dryer off the counter, and it fell into her pack. That was a clear sign that she had to take it, even if most hotels have hairdryers. The curling iron and the other stuff didn't fall out, so that was a sign she had to take them too. Whoever designed bug-out kits must not have had hair.

Tex made a move toward Ria, kicking Audrey in the process.

"Ow." Audrey drew up, items spilling out of her open pack for a second time.

Ria gripped her radio. "You cross me COW-BOY, and you're dead."

"And I'll be over you like stink on a skunk." Tex faked to the right, lurched left, and caught Ria off guard. He snatched the radio. "Do something useful like covering us."

Audrey climbed back over Ria and settled into her spot. Flustered, she turned to face the back of the bus, worried the driver would yell at them to stay in their seats.

Lee pulled out his netbook and brought it out of hibernation mode. He attached a data cord from the computer to Audrey's radio. He typed a command sequence and pressed Execute. Numbers began dancing across the screen.

"What's that?" Ria whispered. She was on her knees looking over the seat in front of Lee, her back to the driver.

"Just do your job. Be wide and dumb, like a wall," Tex said.

"You mess with me again and I'll…I'll…bring Eric Little back here."

"Pleeeese," Audrey said. "We're all on the same team now. Can't we get along?" She sensed Tex was insecure around Ria. He didn't hate her, even though he acted like he did. He was afraid of her. They were too much alike.

"Just because MOLECHECK assigned her to Alpha team doesn't mean she needs to know everything we're doing," Tex grumbled.

"Need to know about what?" Ria demanded.

"If she's on the team, she has to know." Audrey felt certain Ria would be on their side when it came to Marvin. After all, Ria had been teamed with him these past few weeks. Audrey looked over her shoulder. Marvin waved. She waved back.

"How do we know if we can trust her? She's a blabbermouth. She'll ruin everything," Tex said.

"I won't." Ria shook her head with growing intensity. "You're the one who's always breaking the rules. You think because you're a boy you can get away with—"

"Easy, Ria." Lee looked up from his laptop. "I'm a guy, and I am sure that's not the reason why I'm on this bus." Lee detached Audrey's radio from the computer and hooked up Ria's. There was no way she was getting it back inside her pack so Audrey hugged it to her chest. She wished Tex hadn't mentioned trust. MOLECHECK trusted them and now they were doing something she suspected MOLECHECK would consider untrustworthy.

"See this number series?" Lee turned the computer toward Audrey and Ria. "It's the encryption code currently loaded in the radio."

"Right, DASH showed us that last week," Ria said.

When the numbers stopped streaming, Lee started typing.

"What are you doing now?" Ria leaned over the back of her seat and over the computer to get a better look at the screen.

"Hey, move the frizz. I can't see." Lee swatted at the curly black veil.

Ria leaned back. "Okay, but what is that?" She put her finger on the screen where a stream of numbers and letters stood out in red. Her silver charm bracelet with about 50 charms dangled in view.

"I'm writing a shadow code to embed in the master code—if I could see."

Ria removed her hand. "Did DASH show you that too?"

"No, I already knew how to do that. Maybe I'm not the best at being a spy, but I'm pretty sneaky when it comes to finding back doors, especially in computers. I'll insert our own code so only we will know how to access the backdoor."

Audrey looked over her shoulder again. "Marvin keeps looking back here."

"Ignore him," Tex said as Lee keyed in his changes. "Hold your horses. What if we could get a hold of Marvin's radio and fix it so we could listen in?"

"Why are you looking at me?" Audrey scrunched down in her seat, seeking the safety of the high back, away from Tex's gaze.

"He's sweet on you." Tex thumped the back of the seat. "Audrey, think of it, we could finally find out what Marvin is up to while we're doing our mission assignments."

"Then you'll have to get me his radio, too." Lee spoke without taking his eyes off his laptop.

"I could tell you some stories about that two-faced—" Ria started.

"You ready to burn a former team member?" Tex interrupted.

"—that knock-kneed rodent? No problem. But why should I help you?"

Audrey looked at Ria in total surprise. Could it be that everyone was right about Marvin, and she was wrong?

After a whispered planning session, Audrey crabbed her way down the aisle. She tapped Marvin on the shoulder and motioned to him to sit with her in an empty row between Alpha and Theta teams. He was back in a flash. Audrey didn't know whether to be relieved or sick that he brought his backpack with the radio. She had planted herself in the aisle seat and smiled half-heartedly at him when he squeezed by to take the window.

"I wanted to thank you again for the wood carving you made for me. It was really sweet." She smiled at Marvin. He stared back at her, like he was waiting for more. Audrey hesitated and then gushed, "Wow, here we are in the finals."

How was she going to pull this off? Despite going over the plan four times at the back of the bus, she was still not comfortable with her mission. She had been avoiding Marvin for the past week. He was probably wondering why she wanted to talk to him now.

"I was hoping to get some advice…"

She pulled the chain of her grandmamma's necklace. She hadn't meant to pull on it so hard. It snapped, sending her necklace flying between their knees.

"My necklace!" Audrey dove for the floor under Marvin's legs. "Don't move." Her hands moved frantically trying to feel for the lost medallion. Instead they landed on the zipper of Marvin's pack. The radio was right on top. All her senses were screaming. This was what she wanted, and yet she felt uncertain. He probably trusted her and wouldn't suspect her for a second. But could she do it? Should she do it? She had been taught to treat others as she would want to be treated. She wouldn't like someone pretending to be her friend and then stealing her radio. She could hear Tex whistling behind her. The team was depending upon her. The medallion glowed against the grimy floor of the bus. Was it a sign? She felt its rough surface under her fingers. What would her grandmamma do?

"Found it." She slid the radio out of the pack and gave it a hard kick toward the back of the bus. She climbed back into her seat, stepping on Marvin's foot in the process. Audrey fixed the clasp before slipping it over her head and then gave him a big smile.

"You wanted to talk to me?" Marvin's voice wavered but his eyes looked hopeful.

"Yes, well, we've been so busy with this training and stuff that I...I...You know how you want to say something, and then when you go to say it—poof—it's out of your head? Poof! Right now, all gone, don't have a clue." Audrey smiled and shrugged her shoulders like this happened to her all the time.

"I tried to talk to you a couple of times, but you're always busy."

"It's a competition. Can't be seen talking to the enemy." Audrey stared past him and out the window.

"What about now?" Marvin leaned in, trying to make eye contact.

"What do you mean what about now?"

"Well, everyone can see you talking to me right now."

"That's the point," Audrey said. "They can see us. We aren't sneaking around behind their backs. So they wouldn't think we are doing anything wrong. Right?"

Marvin looked at her like she had lost her mind, or at the very least was up to something. Think of something to say, she heard the voice inside of her screaming. She needed to get the focus off of her and back on to Marvin.

"What do you like to do for fun?"

Marvin was off, launching into an in-depth -explanation of his favorite topic. Himself. Audrey stared as his mouth moved up and down and wondered what was taking Lee so long. She was going to have to keep Marvin distracted a little while longer.

"...Maybe we could get together?"

"Sure, I..." Audrey felt a hard object slam into the back of her heel and then bounce. Out of the corner of her eye, she saw the radio slide under the seats across the aisle. The radio was back, and she had missed it.

"I love dancing." She sprang from her seat and twirled in the aisle. "I can do the splits. Wanna see?" Before Marvin could answer, Audrey hit the floor and stretched her left arm toward her toes in a perfect arch, her head resting on her leg and her eyes scanning for the radio. She spotted it wedged under the metal footrest. She stretched forward, grabbed and slid it underneath her seat. Eric was clapping as she popped back into a standing position.

"That was amazing," Marvin said, clapping too.

"I'm so embarrassed." Audrey covered her face and ducked down behind the seat in front of her. She jammed the radio back under the flap of Marvin's pack.

"Sorry," she said bumping against him as she stood.

Marvin had a confused grin on his face. "Strawberries?" he asked in a squeaky voice, sniffing her hair.

Audrey wanted to run. Away from both Marvin and Eric. Instead, she stood, clasped Marvin's hand and shook it several times. "I guess we should get back to our teams. Good luck this week." She rushed toward the back of the bus. Her face burned. Tex was staring at her, a small smile forming as Marvin called out to her.

"Hey! Maybe we could get together in Ivanistan and do something, like, maybe, like take a boat ride on the Potomac?"

— • — • • • — • • • — — • — — — — — • •

Memo for the Record
Date/Time: 7 AUG/1400Z
To: FBI Headquarters
From: Intel Center Headquarters
Re: Special Requirements – DC Training Exercise

Appreciate the Bureau's support for training Junior Spy recruits. Per earlier discussion, we have counter-intelligence concerns about one of the recruits. We will require special focus on her movements the entire time she is deployed to DC.

Your points of contact in the field will be Agents SPOT and TRAIL. They have been fully read into the counterintelligence operation and are cleared for classified information up to the Top Secret, ULTIMATE level.

Going Operational

The bus entered Washington, D.C. during mid-morning traffic. It turned and twisted through the streets, finally making a hard right into a parking garage. Down they went, the wheels screaming in the corkscrew ram, slamming to a stop right before a wall. Tex jumped out of his seat to be the first off the bus, excitement surging through him. He reached the front just in time to see the driver hit a button on the control panel and the wall opened.

The homeroom instructors stood in the shadows of the loading facility waiting for them. MOLECHECK passed out room keys and envelopes. Tex opened his and found maps of Georgetown, a historic neighborhood in Washington D.C., along with a written schedule for meal times and due dates for their assignments.

"Your first assignment in Ivanistan is to select two sites, one for a dead drop and the other for an agent meeting." MOLECHECK waved one of the street maps. "Before dinner tonight, I expect complete casing reports, showing the exact location of agent meeting sites with photographs and drawings of the area for the ops meetings."

"Wahoo, we finally get to hit the streets." Tex headed for the door.

MOLECHECK stopped him. "Choose your locations carefully. Make sure they are easy to get in and out of so you don't get trapped, that they offer some privacy and that you have a good reason for being there. As we discussed before, bathrooms are bad, parks with lots of trees are good. Choose poorly, and you may get ambushed, or worse."

"These rules," Ria grumbled, waving the paper like it would knock the words right off the page. "They are worse than my parents. 'Do this,' 'Don't do that,' and 'Don't even think about it.'" Tex frowned. He suspected Ria was all talk. She was the hall monitor type that he hated.

Tex led Audrey and Ria in search of their rooms, buried in one of the musty halls.

The corridor was dark and smelled like a chemical version of a pine tree. There were no pictures on the walls, just door after drab door with metal numbers.

"Where do you think we are?" Audrey asked.

"It looks a lot like the Watergate Building," Ria said. "I was here once before with my parents. There was a famous break-in here a long time ago, and a spy got caught. It caused a big scandal, and President Nixon was impeached."

"Cool," Tex said. He was in a spy nest.

"Not cool," Audrey said. "It's a dump." Tex held a door open while Audrey dragged her pack into her assigned room.

Ria barreled in after her, purposely knocking into him with her pack. "I'll bet you're the next spy to get caught for doing something dumb."

Tex growled. He'd show Ria not to mess with him.

"Is this a real hotel?" Audrey scrunched her nose. The closet-sized room was packed with two rollaway beds and one small desk to share. Tiny gym lockers were the only places to stuff the costumes, wigs and assorted personal items each of them had brought. There were no windows, and the bathroom was down the hall. She lifted the bedspread. Tex suspected she was checking for signs of bugs.

"Aud, don't worry. We're going to be on the streets most of the time," Tex said. Still he hoped he had a better room assignment. His was somewhere further down the corridor.

"MOLECHECK said it was a safe house." Audrey turned her pack upside down and shook her clothes and hair products across her bed and onto Ria's.

"With you here, no one's safe." Ria flopped on top of her bed.

"Get off my wigs, you're crushing them."

"Then get them off my bed." Ria threw several items to the floor. "I can barely move in here. Keep your mess to yourself."

"Ahh, pardon me," Tex said, catching a black wig.

"What do you want?" Ria groaned. "To move in, too?"

Tex hesitated. "I need to talk to Audrey. Alone."

"I'm on the team too. Spill it!" Ria said.

Tex double-checked the hallway before stepping into the room. He closed the door. "We've got to keep an eye on Marvin. He's up to something."

"Yeah, I know all about the bug." Ria yawned.

Audrey used her wig to swat at something crawling on the nightstand.

"You're bluffing," Tex said.

Ria yawned a second time. "You guys think you're the only ones with problems caused by EAGLE-EYES? Wrong. It would take days to tell you all the times Marvin messed things up, making me look bad. So I repeat, what do you want?"

"We have site casings today," Tex said. "I overheard Marvin say he is going to start at the Georgetown Park Mall. Lee and I thought we should all split up. We'll take the first shift. Audrey, you and Ria can watch him after lunch. That way we all have time to do our assignments."

"Two-person surveillance teams? That won't work. He'll spot us in seconds," Ria said. "Who came up with that dumb idea? Let me guess. You?"

Tex clenched his jaw. He'd had enough of this frizz brain. "Look Ria, I should be the one madder'n a wet hornet. You stranded me remember? Not the other way. I didn't ask you to be on this team."

"And I didn't ask—"

Ria shot off the bed, as Audrey wedged herself between them. The smell of strawberries distracted him enough to make the anger surging inside him switch off.

"Guys, please. We've got to work together. Would it make any difference if Ria and I took the first shift?"

Tex felt sorry for Audrey. She had to live with Ria. That'd be like sleeping with a bull while wearing red pajamas.

"It's still a dumb plan," Ria said. Her curls lashed dangerously around her.

"Dumb is good. Who'd expect that?" Audrey said.

"Yeah, who?" Ria said, making Audrey flush with the implied criticism.

"Pipe down, Ria. I came to talk about the radios," Tex wanted to say his bit and get out there. "Lee didn't program Marvin's like he did ours."

Ria eyeballed Tex with suspicion.

"It wouldn't have worked to put Marvin on our net." Tex grinned. "If you were going to do something sneaky, would you broadcast it over the radio?"

"No. I'd do what DASH taught us, turn all electronics to sleep mode," Ria said.

"Right. So would Marvin. Lee switched the circuits. Now, when Marvin turns off his radio, he activates the frequency that our radios are on, in a send-only mode."

"Won't he hear us talking and stuff?" Audrey asked.

Tex shook his head. "Lee turned Marvin's radio into a hot mike. We can hear him, but he can't hear us."

"At least Lee has some brains," Ria said.

"Aud, where's your radio?" Tex asked, teeth clenched, flattening her other wig as he sat down next to her.

"This button is for our official Alpha team communications." Tex pointed to the largest button on the radio. "But if you press the smaller button next to it two times, it switches over to our private network. You need to keep them straight. You don't want CONTROL and MOLECHECK listening in."

Audrey grabbed a pen and drew a smiley face on the second button. "There, now I can tell them apart."

Ria rolled her eyes. Tex wished Ria would give Audrey half a chance.

— • — • • • — • • • — — • — — — — — • •

Memo for the Record
Date/Time: 3 AUG/0200Z
To: CONTROL
From: SECURITY
Re: Unauthorized Access

The cleaning crew discovered a small compact in the corner of the Instructors' room and alerted Security. Rather than being a lost item, it appears to have been deliberately placed to blind Surveillance Camera 837.

Investigation indicates the top half of mirror was positioned on the focal point of the security camera mounted in the ceiling, reflecting it into the bottom mirror and then toward the window. Review of the surveillance monitor indicates the mirror created a blind spot, obscuring one computer station in the center of the room.

Security checked the tapes for a time stamp when the last authorized personnel left the room. We discovered the rotational motor for Security Camera 224 (hallway) disabled and therefore cannot confirm movement in the corridor for a 24-hour period. Manual log of the Instructors' room indicates BULLDOG secured room at 2010 hours.

Assessment: This breach requires skills far beyond those of the new recruits.
NOTE: Pale blue compact with purple and pink fake jewels, DNA match with Recruit MIND-READER. Security is checking video logs of all her movements over past 5 days. Unable to question MIND-READER because she is TDY with Alpha team on the Training Final Exercise.

Loose Lips

It was an hour later when the team met up with MOLECHECK. He had changed his clothes and was now wearing a tie with sharks swimming on a blue background.

"I want to remind all of you this area is a popular spot for several other agencies' training exercises. Stay alert and watch for surveillance nets. Don't assume all surveillance is on you. Be sure it's yours before you cancel an agent meeting or do something to call attention to yourself. It's messy when we have to pull you out."

Audrey felt for her necklace and twisted the chain.

"If the locals find your actions suspicious they will call the police. Get arrested and you will be eliminated from the program. Two years ago an entire team was picked up for loitering in a residential neighborhood. One of the neighbors thought they were buying drugs. I expect nothing less than great work from you. Good luck today."

The team left the building one by one through an underground tunnel that deposited them at various unmarked doors. Audrey's route took her onto the street through a pet store. A minute later, she saw Tex emerge from an apartment building. Audrey tried to blend in with the activity on the street. Just another kid with a backpack. Nothing suspicious about that. Taking completely different routes, Audrey and Ria headed for the Georgetown Mall.

"MIND-READER and PUZZLE-GIRL, this is COW-BOY." Audrey heard her radio crackle to life as she rode the escalator to the second level of the mall. She pushed her ear buds in tighter to make sure no one else could hear. "Time to dance with the knock-kneed rodent," Tex signed off.

Audrey didn't like the name Ria had for Marvin, but Tex and Lee thought it was perfect. The sentence was the signal to switch over to their private frequency. Lee reminded them there should be some chatter on the training channel since MOLECHECK would be listening.

The mall had an open atrium, giving Audrey a clear view down to the lower levels. Ria stood by the popcorn stand on the first floor. Her hair was now blond and tied back in a ponytail. She wore a light blue beret and glasses, and she carried several shopping bags. Her look blended in with the other shoppers. Audrey smiled. The beret came from her disguise collection. Ria could never pass for being French—her walk was completely wrong—but it did make her look older.

"I've spotted the rodent on the lower level, near Stuff'n Things for Pets. Can one of you get in closer?" Tex said.

"COW-BOY, this is our shift. We've got it handled. Out." Audrey watched Ria pay for her popcorn, thinking the beret should be tilted a bit more to one side for the right effect.

"I'll watch the exit door on the lower level. COW-BOY, Out."

Tucking in between a pair of ficus trees, Audrey saw Marvin walk past Ria and continue down the line of fancy clothing stores, not even pretending to window shop. Ria followed at a distance. Audrey heard the familiar jingle of Ria's charm bracelet. Marvin stopped and spun around in Ria's direction. Had he heard her bracelet too?

Ria let the popcorn fall. It hit the ground, scattering everywhere. Her wig hid her face as she stooped to pick it up. Marvin darted down a narrow corridor toward the restrooms and payphones. Audrey no longer had a visual. Seconds ticked by.

"I got it. I told you I got it," Marvin said into Audrey's earpiece. He must have switched his radio to off. Off for the instructors, but on for Alpha team.

"Everything, names, parents, addresses. No more Junior Spies. It will shut the program down forever. Will that make you happy?" Audrey sensed a combination of frustration, fear and anger. "Yeah, I can meet tomorrow. Where? Okay. See you there."

Audrey guessed Marvin was on the phone. But with whom? What did he mean, shut down the program? She heard metal slam against metal, and a second later Marvin stormed out into the mall, his head and shoulders hunched as if he carried something heavy. He headed for the exit.

Tex popped up on the net. "It worked. The rodent did what we planned."

"That slime-ball is going to expose our program. Somehow he's stolen the personnel files, the ones with our true names," Ria said.

Audrey felt a sudden urge to protect Marvin. Was it because he liked her or because she sensed something was deeply wrong with him and he needed help? Marvin stealing top-secret documents didn't feel right. "He must have had help from someone with access to the files, someone with a grudge," Audrey said. "Someone like BULLDOG. What do you think, COW-BOY?"

"COW-BOY's not in charge. We should be following the rodent to see where he goes next," Ria said, clearly irritated by Tex's continued monitoring of their operation.

"Rodent back on the streets," Tex said. "I'm on him. We can't lose him now."

— • — • • • — • • • — — • — — — — — • •

Memo for the Record
Date/Time: 7 AUG/1630Z
To: MOLECHECK
From: CONTROL
Re: Operation Handcuffs

The FBI surveillance team selected Alpha team recruits as their targets for Day 2 of the Final Exercise. Provide to me by close of business today copies of their casing reports. The FBI coordinator advised their arrest would be videotaped for you to review how they handle the stress and stick to their cover.

The Break In

Tex made his decision after his second hotdog. They had been trading positions and switching up their disguises just like VIOLET had taught them, changing shoes or turning a shirt inside out while tracking Marvin all morning. Marvin had no idea he was being followed. That was the good news. The bad news was they still didn't have a clue as to what he planned to do next.

After the phone call, Marvin had moved about Georgetown, looking at sites, making drawings, and taking photos. It could be for the final exercise. Or it could be in preparation for his other meeting. There was no way they could be sure. Tex was going to have to convince the others that tracking Marvin was more important than finishing their casing reports. Tex switched to Alpha's private net. "The rodent's still in the restaurant."

Audrey's voice came over the radio. "You want us to take over so you can get your final assignment done?"

"I've been thinking, maybe it's more important to stick with Marvin," Tex said.

"What do you mean?" Ria cut in.

"You heard what he said. He's fixin' to expose the program." Tex had a hard time controlling the anger building inside of him after playing cat-and-mouse all day.

"But if you don't do the casings, you'll fail the final exercise," Audrey said.

"If there is no program, it doesn't matter," Tex said.

Audrey keyed in. "I agree it's important to keep the you-know-who in sight. But Lee and I can take over. We've finished our reports…sort of."

"It's not enough to watch him. We've got to stop him." The net went quiet. Tex knew they were thinking about what this meant. What would happen if they didn't complete the last assignment? Would MOLECHECK throw them out immediately, or would he give them a chance to explain?

Tex had already asked himself these questions a thousand times. Common sense told him there would be no second chances but his gut felt different. Tex wanted to be certified more than anything in the world. Spy work was even better than the thrill of racing. He had loved the training. Okay, maybe not the papers and reading so much, but the rest of it. His ma had told him for as long as he could remember to follow his dreams. If he were passionate about something, he would find a way to make it happen. But if he wasn't certified, he didn't have a chance. Somehow, he had to change the rules, and make them play his game.

Audrey triggered the radio. "We need to tell MOLECHECK. There's something else going on. Why would Marvin want to expose the program?"

"All MOLECHECK will do is throw the rodent out with all the evidence he needs to shut down the program, and we'll make it easier by making sure he gets an early bus home," Tex said. "We need to stop him. It's time to fish or cut bait."

"Without any proof? I don't see how," Lee keyed in for the first time.

"Confirm location, L-Man," Tex said.

"Inside the restaurant, behind a large potted fern."

Tex looked across the street. Through the large restaurant window, half hidden by a fern, he saw a Sikh Indian, traditional turban and all. "Is that you in the navy turban?"

"VIOLET said it was a good way to draw attention away from my Asian features. I even put on some aftershave–Indian Nights. I think it's distracting the waitress."

"Lee's right, we need concrete proof." Tex kicked the side of a garbage can, wishing it were EAGLE-EYES's weasel face.

"COW-BOY, get a grip. People are looking at you," Ria said.

Tex hadn't realized Ria was so close. He spotted her waiting at a bus stop across the street and shook his fist.

"Guys in prep school uniforms don't attack garbage cans or threaten innocent bus riders," Ria shot back over the radio.

"So what do we do?" Audrey asked.

"If I knew, I'd be doing it and not standing here trying to blend in with a hotdog cart." Tex realized he was mad as a mule and kicking on his friends. But his chance at his dream job was slipping away. "PUZZLE-GIRL, you're the brain. What do you think?"

"Glad you finally realized it, and I have an idea."

Tex could see her hopping up and down across the street. Maybe her frizzy hair was disguised, but not her annoying habit of bouncing around.

"If EAGLE-EYES is going to pass a large quantity of information, he must have it on him or in his room. We steal it as evidence," Ria said.

"It's probably digital, on his computer or a removable drive," Tex said.

"What if we get caught in his room?" Audrey asked.

"How do we even get into his room?" Ria countered.

"Ah, I have the solution," Lee said. "I have his key."

"How'd you do that?" Tex was impressed. Lee was busy as a hound in flea season.

"Ah, well, uh, I went to the front desk and pretended to be him. Told them I left my key in the room," Lee stammered. "Lousy security."

"What if it's not in his room?" Tex asked, already spinning out a mental ops plan.

"Then you mug him," Lee said, making Tex laugh.

"What about BULLDOG?" Audrey said.

"We're talking about EAGLE-EYES," Ria said. "Focus."

"I know he's involved in this. EAGLE-EYES couldn't do this by himself. I get this feeling from BULLDOG like he's a lion lying in wait for lunch. Why don't we break into his room, too?"

"When are you going to stop standing up for EAGLE-EYES?" Ria demanded. "Or maybe you're on his side?"

"Watch it, PUZZLE-GIRL," Tex warned. "MIND-READER is solid, and you can take that to the bank."

"My mom says, 'Trust but verify,'" Audrey said.

Tex groaned. Audrey was not helping herself or him. He needed her to keep Ria under control. "Aud, we need to keep our focus on Marvin," There was no response from Audrey.

Tex made the team assignments. The three of them would do the break-in while Lee stayed on Marvin's tail.

Tex should have been happy, but something didn't feel right. Audrey's doubts bothered him. Was this bigger than Marvin? And Lee...for a lab rat, he sure got around...the red zone at spy school and now Marvin's room key. He's a right three-jump cowboy. What had he been planning to do with it?

Marvin's room was located two doors down the hall from Tex's. The key Lee supplied slipped in, and the door unlocked. Even though he pretended otherwise, Tex was as worried as Audrey about getting caught. He slapped black tape over the latch so it wouldn't lock and make noise when the door closed. Tex scanned the room for hiding places, while Audrey photographed the placement of every item, so Marvin's room could be put back exactly the way they found it. Ria stood guard outside.

"We need to keep this under 15 minutes. Lee has Marvin covered, but we don't know when his roommate will be back." Data files could be stored on a computer, a removable drive, on CDs or DVDs. They could be hidden in concealment devices, like hollowed out books or Coke cans with secret compartments. Overwhelmed by the possibilities, Tex double-checked his watch.

It felt like forever before Audrey signaled she was finished and switched places with Ria. Tex started his search with a laptop on a rickety desk, while Ria examined Marvin's bug-out pack. Tex tapped the keyboard. The clock in the upper corner tracked the minutes. He couldn't let the weasel outsmart him over a little thing like a password. What would a guy like him use? He tried his name, forward and then backward. When that failed, he tried RODENT just for fun. Then he typed EAGLE-EYES. Dead end. Dang.

Tex noticed Ria was working the room in a grid system. She was annoying, but thorough. He doubted Marvin would be that careful. He'd use something obvious. Marvin never talked about brothers or sisters, let alone pets. What about hobbies? All Marvin talked about was spying. How about spy words? He typed in DEAD DROP. COMMO. SURVEILLANCE. He tried again. SPYMASTER. What about famous spies? Benedict Arnold. No. Mata Hari. No. What about movie spies? FOR YOUR EYES ONLY. And then it clicked: BOND, JAMES BOND.

"I'm in!" Tex's spirits swarmed like a beehive before diving. He searched the hard drive and the history files. "Looks like he has a removable drive. He transferred a large amount of data early this morning." Tex swore.

"Can you capture it?" Ria asked.

"The guy's smarter than I thought. He's erased the files, even the back-up ones most people don't even know about," Tex said.

Audrey stuck her head in. "Fifteen-minute mark."

"I need more time. I want to copy his email file."

"How much?" Ria asked.

"Five minutes…maybe more."

"Okay, but I'm starting cleanup."

Ria moved around the room, using the images from Audrey's camera. She verified that the locker looked how it had before she opened it. She moved on to the bed, adjusting a suitcase under it. "Look at this." Ria removed a photo wedged between the mattress and the wall.

Tex looked away from the data streaming across Marvin's computer. It showed a man standing on a dock in front of a sailboat. He was wearing a cap and leaning against the boat in a relaxed pose. The owner? "Take a picture of it," he told Ria.

A noise outside made both Ria and Tex freeze. Audrey was tapping a series of signals on the door. Then voices and the sound of Audrey sobbing. Tex looked at Ria. They were so busted.

— • — • • • — • • • — — • — — — — • •

Memo for the Record
Date/Time: 7 AUG/1715Z
To: CONTROL
From: SPOT, Security
Re: Recovered Concealment Device

Housekeeping turned over one of the missing classified concealment devices today. The Soda Can concealment device was discovered hidden behind a locker in Boys Bunkhouse B. The locker is registered to recruit COW-BOY.

23

Hidden Codenames

Audrey was the last to arrive at the Georgetown Public Library, the agreed upon rendezvous site. It had taken longer than she expected to get rid of Marvin's roommate Trevor. First she had to convince him that he didn't really need to go into his room and then get him to look the other way away so Tex and Ria could escape. All of them would have been caught if Tex hadn't remembered to remove the black tape covering the lock. Ria said that's how the Watergate burglars were caught. The tape gave them away.

She found Ria and Tex on the second floor back by the books on local interest, huddled over their laptops. Lee was still keeping an eye on Marvin, who was now in the group room with his team working on their reports.

"Look at this," Ria said. Tex had digitally enhanced the photo Ria had found, and Audrey could barely make out the name painted on the side of the sailboat: *Ku Bark*. "The boat is registered at a marina in Virginia. The owner is a guy by the name of Matthew Russell."

"What's Marvin's last name, and where does he live?" Tex asked.

"Ames. He's from Oregon," Audrey said."

"Maybe it's a dead-end," Ria said. She closed her eyes and sat unusually still.

"*Ku Bark* is a weird name," Audrey said. "I don't know why, but I have a feeling there's more."

She picked up the printed copy of the picture and stared into the man's face. He vaguely resembled Marvin. There was something in his eyes, intensity...anger.

"Nothing in Google searches on *Ku Bark* except the boat," Ria said. "Russell is a common name. Too common. There must be a million hits."

"I found a few saved histories on his hard drive he didn't erase," Tex said. "Need something specific?"

"Anything connecting Marvin to this guy or the boat," Ria said.

Tex searched the files he had copied to his laptop. "I remember an email from Matthew to Marvin about reconnecting."

"Nothing more? The photo tells us there's a connection, but maybe he's just a family member," Ria said. Her frown deepened.

"Then why would Marvin hide the photo?" Audrey sensed a missing piece. She closed her eyes and visualized Marvin, his room, his gift to her, the photo, and the expensive boat. Behind her, she could hear a tinkling from Ria's bracelet. Tinkle tinkle. Tinkle twinkle. Twinkle, ching, chong. The sound of bells rang in Audrey's head while her thoughts jumped and rang and bounced. Suddenly, an idea sprung from the deepest part of her brain.

"KU-BARK! It's like our codenames." Audrey looked at Ria. She was afraid Ria would tell her to stop being silly, they didn't have the time for it. But when she said the words "Ku Bark," they rolled off her tongue like LAB-MAN and MOLECHECK. It tasted the same. How could she explain that to Ria without being laughed out of the library?

But Ria didn't say a word. Instead, she started typing KU-BARK, with a hyphen. Two hits came up.

Audrey bent over Ria's shoulder scanning the text. The first item was a newspaper article, dated 10 years ago. An unnamed source had accused the U.S. government of exploiting children, turning them into assassins and criminals under the false pretense of training them as spies. The codename of the program was KU-BARK. Audrey gasped. Was this their program? The identity of the source was being protected because he feared for his life. His goal was to shut down the program because, in his words, it was illegal and immoral.

Audrey's radio squawked. The librarian at the reference desk shot her a nasty look. Audrey popped behind the bookshelf. "Check, MIND-READER," she whispered.

"LAB-MAN here. MOLECHECK is looking for you guys. Reports are due in 10 minutes." Audrey's heart sank. There was no way they could make it from the library to the Watergate in 10 minutes. Not to mention the problem of unfinished reports.

"MOLECHECK wants to see us," Audrey said, rejoining the group, "Now what?"

"What we're trained to do," Tex said. "Deny everything. Lee you're gonna need to provide some diversion."

Audrey waited outside the door, listening as Lee asked MOLECHECK question after question about his reports and his upcoming agent meeting. When he finally ran out of questions, Audrey knocked and entered. Lee looked relieved and quickly left the cramped room in the basement of the Watergate. She closed the door behind her. Tex wanted her to delay MOLECHECK long enough so that he and Ria could complete their reports. She wanted to get inside MOLECHECK's head.

"What's going on MIND-READER?"

MOLECHECK's eyes twinkled.

"Can I ask you something?" Her voice quivered.

MOLECHECK studied her. "What?"

"Does our program have a codename?" Audrey held her breath. She focused all of her senses on MOLECHECK. She listened to his breathing and the little-too-long pause.

"What?" MOLECHECK showed no emotion.

"Does it have a codename?"

"Yes."

"What is it?" Audrey said.

"You're not cleared for that information."

Audrey fought back the impulse to argue. She had this odd sense that she was talking to her mom, and her mom was once again evading her questions. "You're not cleared," sounded too much like "I don't want to talk about this." She closed her eyes. This was MOLECHECK, not her mother. She focused on MOLECHECK once more, listening to him breath in and out, like he had just run a mile.

She opened her eyes. "Is it KU-BARK?"

MOLECHECK stared intently at her.

"Is it?" she asked again.

His mouth said no. His eyes said yes.

— • — • • • — • • • — — • — — — — — • •

Memo for the Record
Date/Time: 7 AUG/0100Z
To: CONTROL
From: MOLECHECK
Re: Stolen Concealment Devices

I confronted COW-BOY this evening on the missing/ recovered concealment devices. He appeared nervous, but surprised and angered by the accusation. I assess he was expecting a different kind of confrontation.

COW-BOY denied taking the concealment devices. He maintained good eye contact with me when being questioned and did not attempt to deflect my questions until I asked him who he thought might have stolen it. He said he did not want to guess because he didn't know. I suggested LAB-MAN. He vouched for the reliability of his teammate.

COW-BOY has strong dissembling skills; he could lie his way out of any situation. I assess that if COW-BOY is not guilty, he knows who is. Either way, his not being more forthcoming makes me question his integrity and suitability.

Decision Hour

Lee passed around a new bag of M&M's as the team sprawled on the king-size bed in his room. Every ops meeting had to have snacks, and he preferred his with peanuts.

"How'd you get this room in the tower anyway?" Ria asked. "Audrey and I have to share a basement space the size of a jail cell. It's even decorated like one. You've got a TV too. No fair."

"Not so loud," Audrey said. "Someone might hear us."

Lee checked his watch. It was after midnight. The regular hotel guests were probably sleeping. MOLECHECK had been caught off guard by Audrey's question about KU-BARK, but not enough that he let them get away with sloppy reports. He had them work well past curfew until the casing reports met his approval, which meant precise locations for agent meetings, with maps, flowcharts and photos. He actually hollered at them several times. Lee felt lousy they had disappointed their mentor.

"It's okay, I'm the only one on this floor. It's practically Siberia." It had been as simple as a few clicks into the master reservations system to get the upgrade for Mr. Todd Splinky. He needed to redirect the conversation. "Why do you think MOLECHECK lied to Audrey about the program's codename?"

"Maybe, it's only a partial lie. DASH said the best deceptions are built on a kernel of truth," Ria said.

Lee's jaw dropped. "Sweet Einstein! You mean, you think we're being trained as assassins?"

"Your brain must have shorted. Have more M&M's. Maybe the story in the paper is a lie, but the codename is real," Ria said.

"How would you prove that hypothesis?" Lee asked.

"Have you been trained to kill anyone this summer? I haven't." Ria let go of a lock of hair. Tex ducked out of the way of the springing projectile. "Except maybe during Crash and Bang. We know we're being trained to be spies and keep secrets."

"Can we get back to discussing the rodent?" Tex said.

"That reminds me." Lee pulled a normal-looking leather briefcase out from under his bed. "I have just what we need to expose him." He opened the flap, fumbled around inside and pulled out a small video camera hidden in a false bottom of the case. "Thanks to MOLECHECK and his equipment closet we can secretly film Marvin when he meets his contact."

"So how do we find out where he's meeting?" Audrey asked.

"Marvin spent a lot of time today along the C&O Canal." Tex grabbed the camera and pointed it at Audrey. She made faces for the camera.

"He also spent time down along the waterfront. Any of those warehouses would be a good place for a private meeting," Ria said.

"Audrey and I will check the canal," Tex said. "Ria, you check out the waterfront, and Lee, you follow Marvin with the camera."

"That puts everyone on the street," Lee said. "Who will track his movements on the map and tell you where to go?"

"Good point. Obviously you're the one to do it," Tex said.

"Sweet." Lee looked around the room. "I can turn this place into a surveillance command center. The 12th floor is high enough. Look." Lee pulled back the floor-to-ceiling curtains. "I have a clear view over Georgetown, a clean audio and video field."

"I still don't understand how you got this room." Ria said.

"It's because he's a boy," Tex grinned. Ria spun on her knees as Tex turned the camera on her. Before the sparks could ignite, Lee threw himself between them. He grabbed the netbook.

"If you guys promise not to kill each other in the next 24 hours, I'll tell you how we can have a live video feed," Lee said, pulling cords out of his backpack. "I'll integrate the video with the audio from the radio through a base station on my laptop. The camera will be our eyes and the radio our ears." The distraction worked. Tex helped Lee clear the desk and set up the equipment.

Audrey rubbed her eyes and yawned. "So the plan is we surveil him while he makes contact?"

"No," Tex said. "We have to stop him from passing information. We'll use video and audio as proof that Marvin tried to pass secrets when we turn him over to MOLECHECK. Agreed?"

"Agreed," Lee and Audrey said in unison.

Tex glared at Ria.

Ria crossed her arms. "What if we get caught before we catch Marvin? We'll miss our final agent meetings. Do you think MOLECHECK will do nothing when we don't show? He'll send people to look for us."

Tex stopped. "I didn't think of that."

"I did," Lee popped up between the desk and wall, a cord in his mouth.

"So?" Tex asked.

Lee grinned. "I swapped MOLECHECK's radio with mine. He was too busy hollering about our reports, he didn't even notice. It's in my backpack, with the battery pack off." Lee glanced at Ria. "It might be useful to have the frequency and code for the instructor net. I'll monitor both nets and alert you if anyone is looking for us."

Tex whistled. "There's no slack in your rope."

"How will you return the radio without being noticed?" Audrey asked.

"The radios all look the same. I doubt he'll even notice. I'll do the swap tomorrow morning during breakfast. You can be my diversion," Lee said.

Ria twirled her curls around her pencil. "I think I'd make a better diversion."

"Hairball here does have a point. Her curls could block the sun," Tex said.

Ria lunged at Tex with a screech.

"No waking the other guests." Tex put his finger to his lips. "We have less than 12 hours to catch a mole."

_ . _ . . . _ . . . _ _ . _ _ _ _ . .

Memo for the Record
Date/Time: 8 AUG/1200Z
To: CONTROL
Info: MOLECHECK
From: Security
Re: Alpha team

Alpha team members COW-BOY, MIND-READER and
PUZZLE-GIRL were observed leaving room 1020 in five-
minute intervals at 0130 hours last night. Room 1020 is
registered to a Todd Splinky. Note to Security. Find out
who he is and why Alpha team was in his room. Behavior
was suspicious. Security will conduct a room search of all
team members once trainees have departed the building
for their field exercise.

Mole Traps

Lee adjusted his glasses and surveyed the equipment on his desk. It was the wee hours of the morning when he had finished setting up the laptop for the video feed from the concealed camera. He had also created a radio base station that allowed him to listen to the Alpha net and other nets operating in the area. He reminded the team over breakfast that if they did not have the video camera, they had to describe to him in detail what they were seeing. Otherwise, he would be blind.

Alpha team left the Watergate with the rest of the teams at precisely 8:30 a.m. Tex wore long shorts and a reversible Hawaiian shirt, with a map of Washington, D.C.

sticking out of his back pocket. A straw hat sat low on his head, hiding his face. Audrey took on the role of a student, wearing lightweight yoga pants, a hooded sweater and a small backpack. Ria transformed herself into a professional office worker in a nondescript blue business suit, her curls temporarily straightened by Audrey's flatiron. Lee felt a twinge of envy, wishing he were on the streets and not in the safety of his room.

He hoped in all the confusion and excitement of the teams leaving, that no one would notice he wasn't there. It was important for MOLECHECK to believe the entire team left on schedule for their final mission. What MOLECHECK wouldn't know was it wasn't the one he had planned for them.

"I'm tracking the rodent up M Street," Ria said softly into her concealed microphone at precisely 8:45 am.

"Roger. All systems a go." Lee confirmed he could hear and see Ria's transmissions. The video quality was good. Marvin was not with his team or in disguise. He wore old jeans, a ratty tee and a baseball cap. He walked with confidence, not even bothering to check if he was being followed. Ria even managed to capture a clean shot of his face.

"Whoa, what's going on out there?" Lee said when Marvin disappeared into a kaleidoscope of colors and images. Lee had warned Ria to walk slow and steady so the briefcase did not shake from side to side. Clearly, she was not going to make his job easy.

"Sorry, making some adjustments. Pantyhose slipping."

"Too much information." Lee hunched over the screen, trying to make sense of the street images coming at him from all angles. "I can't help you if I can't see where you're going or the target. Try to get that bag under control."

"Aye, aye Captain." The video image steadied. "He's making a left. Can't see the street name yet. This skirt's too tight. I can't move…oops."

Lee groaned, as Marvin became a blur again.

"Looks like its 30th Street. He's heading for the waterfront."

Suddenly an ear-splitting screech shot through Lee's head, making him pitch his headset. What was that? Some kind of electronic interference? He watched the video feed, which continued with no interruption. Marvin was still on the move, and he was picking up the pace, making the video image jump more frequently as Ria tried to stay behind him. Lee slipped his headphones back on, relieved the screeching had stopped.

"We have a visual." Tex cut in over Ria on the microphone. "MIND-READER and I are in an alleyway. The rodent practically ran over us."

"Omigosh!" Audrey's voice popped up on the net.

"No eyes, MIND-READER. Talk to me," Lee said with a calm he did not feel.

208

"Sorry, a gust of wind knocked the rodent's hat off."

"Thanks for the weather report. Tell me why I should care."

"Wait a sec. I want to catch it."

"The hat?" Lee asked.

"The paper. I don't think he realized he dropped it when he grabbed for his hat."

Lee could hear Audrey breathing hard. She had forgotten to turn off her microphone. He then heard her whispering to Tex, something about moving his big oaf.

"Got it," rang through his earpiece.

"I'm still blind. What do you have, MIND-READER." Lee was getting impatient.

"It's an address," Audrey said. "485 Canary Street."

"Wait!" Lee said. Where was Ria? "PUZZLE-GIRL, do you read me?" Nothing. "COW-BOY? MIND-READER...R...R?"

Lee held his breath. Why had they all stopped talking? He could see Ria's camera was still on, but it had been focused on what looked to be the side of a building. She wasn't moving.

"Talk to me PUZZLE-GIRL," Lee pleaded.

"NIGHT-WIND is talking to EAGLE-EYES. But it looks like the he's waving her off. He's coming back past me. I think he's heading toward the Watergate. COW-BOY and MIND-READER are on him."

Lee was beyond frustrated. Where did Hannah come from? Now he really wished he were out on the street with them. If they ever got through this, he was going to drill it into them to describe in sharp detail, not chat, when doing technical surveillance. He was in control now, and they needed to listen to him.

"COW-BOY, MIND-READER?" No response. Marvin was backtracking. Had their cover been blown? WHY WAS NO ONE RESPONDING? Had Hannah seen them and warned Marvin? He was beginning to hate being in charge of surveillance.

— · — · · · — · · — — · — — — · ·

In an eighth floor office opposite the Watergate Hotel, an FBI technician stretched. It had been a long morning, tracking the radio transmissions and movements of the Junior Spy recruits. He was having some technical interference. Someone was transmitting on an unauthorized frequency. The transmission was coded, so he couldn't read it. He tried to knock the transmitter off the frequency by pinging it. Each time he sent an ear splitting blast, the transmitter went down, but then popped back up. Someone sure can take abuse, the technician mused.

The FBI agent grabbed his phone and hit speed dial. "Agent TRAIL?"

"You got 'im."

"I'm picking up an unauthorized transmitter and receiver. Check it out."

"Where is it?" TRAIL said over the phone.

"From your operation's base. Maybe it's your mole."

"On it." The receiver went dead.

Grand Theft

Audrey and Tex tailed Marvin back into the Watergate. Tex insisted on staying tight to their rabbit, but Audrey sensed that something was not right. She pulled Tex behind a large potted palm, right before CONTROL nabbed Marvin in the lobby.

"EAGLE-EYES, last I checked you were supposed to be conducting a countersurveillance run to confirm the FBI isn't tailing you."

"I forgot something?" Marvin tried to break free of CONTROL.

"Work on remembering out in the field," CONTROL said.

Audrey made like a statue while CONTROL walked Marvin out the door. Audrey started to follow Marvin once CONTROL disappeared, but Tex stopped her.

"Now's our chance to finish the search of Marvin's room."

"But Lee said to stay with Marvin," Audrey said.

"Lee's not in charge."

"What if we can't find Marvin again?"

Tex pulled out his radio. "LAB-MAN, have PUZZLE-GIRL track the rodent. He just left the hotel. We're signing off for a bit." Tex turned his radio off without waiting for a response. "Let's go."

The hallway was empty outside Marvin's room. Once in, Audrey fumbled for the light but Tex blocked her. He pointed to a gap under the door where light filtered in. It took a few moments for her eyes to fully adjust before she could begin searching the room. The open suitcase, filled with clothes, was the first thing she saw. Was he planning an early departure?

Tex picked a piece of paper off the desk. "What do you think this means?

Meet me at the dock.

Smooth sailing ahead.

"I need some light." Audrey grabbed for a penlight at the same time as Tex, knocking over a glass of water and drenching the note.

"Great, now look what you've done."

Audrey was about to apologize when Tex clamped his hand over her mouth. "Someone's coming," he whispered. She grabbed the wet paper and slid under Marvin's bed, Tex was right behind her. The penlight forgotten on the desk sent small pinpricks of light all over the room.

"The light." Tex started to move, but Audrey was faster. She slid back under the bed as the handle turned. Tex threw his body on top of the penlight just before Marvin entered the room. The overhead light flipped on. Audrey could see Marvin's feet pacing back and forth in front of the bed. He was mumbling to himself. There was a sound of a zipper, and then a series of thuds from something hitting the mattress above them. A backpack dropped to the floor inches from her nose. She heard the rustling of curtains and then the slam of the locker door. Marvin's watch beeped. There was an exasperated sigh and the click of a door closing. He had forgotten to turn off the light.

Audrey wiggled out from under the bed. Tex switched off the penlight.

"Look," Audrey said. A puddle of water had formed under Marvin's desk. Marvin had been looking for something important enough that he hadn't noticed. Tex searched the desk and locker while Audrey searched the bed and the open suitcase. There was a card hidden under one of Marvin's shirts. She opened it. It was a birthday card. The kind that would have been given to a much younger kid. It was a bear driving a steam engine. Inside the inscription read,

I promise to make it up to you one day. – Dad.

"Someone's controlling Marvin," Audrey said. "I can't explain why, I just feel it."

"What makes you think he's not playing you? All of this could be a set-up. He's so crooked you can't tell from his tracks if he's coming or going."

Audrey stared at the soggy note still clutched in her hand. She held it up, surprised the ink had not run. She stopped. Could it be?

"We have to go to my room. Now."

Once safely inside, Audrey grabbed her hairdryer while Tex spread the wet paper on the desk. It only took seconds for the hot air to reveal traces of another set of sentences between the visible lines.

Tex gave a low whistle, "He used invisible ink."

"My sense is he didn't write this. Someone else did. Probably the guy in the picture, Matthew what's-his-face." Audrey held the hairdryer over a small area of the paper trying to bring back all the words. "Look."

Tex leaned over her shoulder and read out loud.

Meet me at the dock.

Board the canal boat at Thomas Jefferson Street, first tour of the day.

Flash-drive in tourist map. Take a seat at the front. Do not leave the boat until the end of the tour.

Emergency fallback meeting, one hour later, at warehouse.

Smooth sailing ahead.

Tex switched on his radio and signaled Ria and Lee, telling them about the note, the flash drive and Marvin's contact plans.

"About time you guys came back on the net," Lee chimed. "I've been filling in the radio silence with the recordings I made from yesterday. I'm running out of filler, and the instructors will start noticing the repeats. Eyes on Marvin?"

"PUZZLE-GIRL's watching him," Tex said.

"You were," Ria popped up on the net. "You saying you lost him?"

"I told you to pick him up." The color drained from Tex's face. Audrey reached for her necklace.

"You did not," Ria shot back.

"I did too," Tex hollered into the radio.

"Maybe I was supposed to relay that message?" Lee said. "Wait a sec. I'm getting static on the instructor net."

The radio went silent.

Audrey could scream. She knew they should have stayed on Marvin.

Tex looked down at his feet. "Sorry, Aud. I guess I got excited and forgot about the plan."

The radio squawked. Lee was back. He sounded panicked. "PUZZLE-GIRL, get off the streets. The Feds are after you."

"Feds?" Audrey asked, keying her radio.

"The FBI. Remember, we're on our final exercise. They're trying to wrap us up. I've been monitoring the instructor net all morning, listening to them pick off one recruit after another. They're looking for PUZZLE-GIRL now."

"Roger," Ria replied over the net. "That might explain a few of the suspicious characters I've been noticing."

"You've been spotted. Move!"

Audrey could hear the sound of running. Ria had forgotten to release the push button of her radio. They couldn't talk on the net until she did. A horn sounded, and wheels screeched. A car door slammed. Then music. Audrey looked over at Tex. He shook his head. What was Ria doing? Minutes passed.

"That was close," Ria said, coming back on to the net.

"What's happening?" Audrey and Tex said into the radio at the same time.

"Feds almost caught me, but I borrowed their car. Do you think they'll mind?"

"Way to go, PUZZLE-GIRL," Tex said, giving Audrey a high-five. "But you might want to ditch it, pronto. That's grand theft auto. Kind of serious if the Feds want to arrest you."

"Not to mention you're not supposed to be driving," Lee chimed in. "Are you CRAZY?"

"Hey, we're in Ivanistan. It's legal. Nobody will be looking for me in a car. I'm going to find the address Marvin dropped. Somewhere on Canary Street. I'll check it out. Signing off."

Audrey was impressed. Ria wasn't timid. She didn't think she'd have the nerve to steal a get-away car. What would her grandmamma say? What would her mom say?

Lee's voice cut through her thoughts. "COW-BOY and MIND-READER, find EAGLE-EYES and try to recover the flash drive."

"Roger," keyed in Tex. "We'll head for the C&O Canal. The note says the rodent needs to be on the first tour."

"One last thing," Lee said. "Don't know if this is important or not, but I haven't heard a peep out of BULLDOG on the instructor net all morning."

Audrey's stomach dropped. That could only mean something was really wrong.

The sign at the Park Station sales booth said the first sailing left in 20 minutes. They decided Audrey would board the boat, and Tex would photograph everything that happened from the towpath.

Audrey was one of the first to board, following the wooden ramp from the towpath down to the boat. The

218

canal was significantly lower than the street level. Audrey guessed years of development had built up Georgetown so the canal seemed to run under the town. She looked downstream, noting the bridges overhead were street level, with cars and people rushing by not even noticing the pretty scene below them. What Audrey noticed most was the stench. The rich, earthy smell of the mud and algae mixed with the sweet perfume of summer flowers, creating an overpowering aroma. It was like August in a bottle. Audrey wished she could enjoy the boat ride and a lazy summer day. But she had a mission.

She selected a seat at the back of the boat and pulled the hood of her blue jacket over her hair, hoping to remain anonymous. She buried her face in a map of Washington, D.C. and waited. Tex was in place, up on the towpath that ran on one side of the canal. He planned on following the boat by taking cover alongside two mules harnessed to the boat. The mules served as the engine and pulled a canal boat weighed down with dozens of tourists.

The boat rocked. Audrey peered around her map in time to see Hannah take a seat several rows in front of her. What was she doing here? Now she'd have to hide from her too. Or, maybe she should sit with her? She was a good friend of Ria's. It would give her a cover to be on the boat. Before she could make up her mind, a large group of tourists climbed on the boat. They took the empty seats in front and behind Hannah. Audrey was angry with herself for her indecision and slumped further down behind her map.

"Welcome Ladies and Gentleman." Once the final group boarded, the round-faced woman dressed in early-American clothing began the tour.

"This is the C&O Canal tour of Old Georgetown. Parents, please make sure your children remain seated throughout the tour. It's a hot day, but I'm sure nobody wants to take a plunge into the canal."

Marvin was the last one to step clear of the ramp, which was promptly removed by one of the workers. He headed down the aisle, pushing past people to the front of the boat. He sat in the second row of benches, on the left. Audrey noticed a man in the front row; seated directly in front of him, turn his head slightly on Marvin's arrival. His face was partially obscured by a scruffy beard and a straw hat, but she was certain it was the man from the picture. The eyes were the same, cold and menacing. Audrey reached for her necklace and said a silent prayer. She needed courage.

The boat lurched forward. Audrey snapped her head to the right. The mules were moving along the towpath. So much for Plan A, getting the flash drive before the cruise started. Trying not to panic, she took a deep breath. The lady seated next to her smiled.

"Don't worry, the boat's perfectly safe." She bounced a toddler on her knee.

Audrey felt more desperate by the second. This was a total mistake. She should have insisted Tex get on the boat and that she monitor the meeting from the path. She had no idea what she should do now. She couldn't use her radio and ask for help because someone might hear her.

The tour guide stood in the middle of the boat, near the opening where the ramp had been removed, retelling the history of Georgetown, not as history, but as a character in a story.

"When I was a little girl, we moved to Georgetown, which was then a new town, started in 1751. My father was in the tobacco business, and Georgetown was the most important port in the area...."

As the cameras clicked, Audrey shifted in her seat to get a better look at Marvin and his contact. They weren't talking to each other. In fact they were acting like they didn't know each other. Marvin looked miserable. Audrey felt faint. She couldn't see their hands. She thought about MOLECHECK's lesson on brush passes and quick encounters. *Never look like you know your contact. Don't talk. Don't make eye contact. Just move your hands*. Marvin might have already made the pass.

There was no time to waste. Audrey stood and headed toward the front. "Marvin, hey, Marvin..." The boat lurched. Audrey felt something block her leg, and she pitched forward. She grabbed for anything to stop her fall, taking the tour guide down with her. She lay there for a moment trapped in the narrow aisle.

"You all right?" Hannah offered her hand but wouldn't let go once Audrey was upright. Two tourists helped the tour guide to her feet. She adjusted her bonnet and attempted to get the story back on track. Marvin turned, surprise and concern flashed across his face. He stepped into the aisle. Was he going to run?

Audrey needed to get control of the situation. "I can't believe it!" she yelled a little too loudly. Shaking off Hannah, she pushed toward him. "I thought you liked me, and I find you here with HER! You were supposed to be taking me on a boat ride."

Marvin froze. He looked toward his contact, but Audrey was already in front of him. She slapped him hard across the face. Startled, he dropped the map he was carrying. A small black object the size of a pack of gum flew out from the pages toward Audrey. By luck or training, her hand managed to wrap around it before it hit the ground. It was the flash drive. With her other hand, Audrey flung the map at Marvin, smacking him for a second time.

"Don't you ever talk to me again!"

Marvin's contact grabbed Audrey toward him.

"Give it to me," he whispered in her ear.

"I have it, Dad." The man released his grip on Audrey, and turned toward Marvin.

"Run!" was the last thing Marvin said to her.

— • — • • • — • • • — — • — — — — • •

FBI agent Phillips keyed his radio. "I want an all-points bulletin out on a Ria Santos, age 13, black hair, 5 foot 3, 100 pounds."

"This is Dispatch. What's the charge? And did I hear that right. Thirteen?"

"Yeah, you heard me," the agent growled. "Car theft."

"Isn't that a federal crime?" the dispatch officer asked.

"You bet it is. It's a federal vehicle."

The delay on the radio was a bit too long. When the dispatcher responded, Agent Phillips thought he could detect a hint of laughter. "Whose federal vehicle?"

"Mine," Agent Phillips barked into the transmitter.

"So a 13-year-old knows how to hot wire a car?" the dispatch asked.

"No, she used the keys."

There was no hint of laughter now. "If I were you, Agent Phillips, I wouldn't be reporting I left my keys in the ignition. That would be negligence. Not theft."

"I want my car back."

"I'll radio around. Informally. Is it one of Intel Headquarters recruits?"

"Yes and she's toast when I catch her. I'll teach her to mess with the Bureau."

A Party of Three

Tex was playing tourist. While the boat was loading, he photographed the arrival of Marvin and the man from the picture. His mission was easy; provide documentary evidence that Marvin-the-weasel was working with someone else and catch the two of them together on film. If anything went wrong, he was responsible for helping Audrey escape.

He keyed Lee on the radio for a check in, but there was no response. Where was Lee?

The boat started moving. They had planned on the guide talking for five or ten minutes before the cruise began, giving Audrey time to confront Marvin and escape.

Obviously, they figured wrong. Tex ran along the towpath and caught up with the mules and their trainer. "Sweet girls you have there."

The trainer, used to tourists being interested in the training regime for the mules, launched into an explanation before Tex even asked. Walking backwards, Tex photographed the mules and trainer as he talked, all while keeping an eye on the boat.

Through the viewfinder he could see a sudden flurry of activity. When a blue blur ran toward the front of the boat, he knew it was time. Audrey was implementing Plan B. He needed a way to reach her. Less than 50 paces away, was one of the canal bridges. Would Audrey be able to move that fast? Tex eyed a coiled rope looped over the mule's harness. Come hell or high water, it would have to do.

As the trainer posed for photos with another tourist. Tex grabbed a pinecone lying on the towpath and jammed it under the mule's harness. "Sorry girl," he whispered. Then he snagged the rope.

The mule immediately objected to the prickly object pressing into her hide. Braying and honking, she threw back her head. She came to a sudden stop, causing the mule in the harness next to her to pull and jerk. The trainer dressed in colonial garb left the photo op to grab for the mule nearest him. He tried to calm her, calling to her by name. He motioned to the boat captain to give him a moment as the boat came to a stop, the bow nearly even with the low bridge.

Perfect. Tex ran.

Inside the boat, the crowd looked on in horror as the jilted girl in the blue hoodie climbed out the forward window.

"She's gonna jump," someone yelled. "Stop her."

Audrey reached for the railing that ran along the length of the boat roof. Tex watched as she struggled to pull herself up, putting one leg over the railing and then the other. Tex reached the bridge and uncoiled the rope, holding it like a lasso. When the front of the boat stopped right before the bridge, he tossed one end to Audrey.

"Knot it around your waist and hang on." Tex dropped to his knees and steadied himself against the safety rail. Audrey grabbed the rope, wrapped it around her tiny waist twice and tied it with a bow.

"I said a knot! That won't hold."

Hannah poked her head out of the window and began making her way onto the roof. "Hang on," Tex yelled. He pulled. She was light, maybe the bow would hold. Hannah grabbed Audrey's leg as she was lifted into the air.

"Don't hurt her," Marvin yelled.

Audrey kicked hard as she tried to pull herself up. Hannah fell back, but not before catching the end of the rope and pulling on the bow, releasing it. Audrey struggled to hang on.

Tex reached down and grabbed her arm, hauling her the final few feet to safety. "Nice going. You knocked Hannah out."

"I didn't mean too." Audrey looked down at the boat. "What's she even doing here?"

"You tell me. Look, we gotta run. Marvin's contact is after us. Did you get it?"

Audrey nodded. They ran from the canal, cutting in between old warehouses while the horse-drawn boat continued under the bridge and floated away. Tex's mind was racing as fast as his heart. They had the flash drive. But what if that wasn't everything? It had been bugging him since he overheard Marvin's phone call. Marvin said he got the rest of it. What if Marvin had already given up some information, like what he tossed over the fence during the crash and bang exercise?

Audrey screeched to a halt.

"Don't stop. They're following us," Tex turned and looked behind them. An ice cream truck moved slowly up the street toward them. There was no sign of Marvin or his contact. Yet.

Audrey pointed to the street sign over their heads. Canary Street.

Tex blinked. There were too many questions and not enough answers. He didn't have time to sort it all out. He needed to act, to make a decision. His gut told him the

Canary warehouse was where Marvin and his contact were headed next.

"Aud, take the flash drive to Lee and meet me back here. I'm going to do a quick check of the address."

"But Ria's doing that."

"If I'm right about Marvin, she's going to need some backup. Run like a prairie fire with a tail wind. Tell Lee to start downloading and assessing the information pronto and whatever you do, don't get caught. And tell him his radio's not working."

"But I need to tell you about Marvin. He said—"

"Later." Tex turned and headed down Canary Street.

"It's his dad," Audrey yelled after him.

Tex darted behind a trash bin, as something white caught his eye. It flashed and then disappeared around a building.

— • — • • • — • • • — — • — — — — • •

The meter attendant walked up to the bicycle messenger standing on the sidewalk alongside the C&O Canal. "Hey, buddy, you can't lock your bike against the parking meters."

The messenger turned around, glared at the attendant and then grinned. "Agent SPOT. Almost didn't recognize you. Nice uniform. You look good as a meter-maid." The bicycle messenger turned his attention back toward the water, watching a boat disappear around the bend in the canal.

"Works well for surveillance. Everyone tries to avoid me. And it beats wearing tight pants." Agent SPOT was glad he didn't have to fit his extra-large body into the spandex bike shorts. He turned to look at the boat as well.

"You getting ready to roll up your target?" the bicycle messenger asked.

"That's your call. You're the FBI," Agent SPOT said.

"We're still watching her. Something odd happened on the canal boat. We're trying to sort that out, with the plan of setting up on her before her 10:30 meeting. We might move it up, though. We're waiting for a decision."

"Don't wait too long. We missed one this morning already. The Asian kid. He was a no-show for his 9:30."

"That big kid? He's hard to miss. I tracked him yesterday. Come to think of it, I haven't seen him today," the FBI agent in bike shorts said.

Agent SPOT grunted in response as the transmitter buzzed in his ear.

"Roger," he responded into the microphone. "Got to go. There's an encrypted signal jamming the airwaves. We've triangulated in on it and are taking it down..."But the agent on the bicycle was already gone, peddling at a breakneck speed along the footpath toward the disappearing boat.

Into the Lair

Lee changed the radio frequency so Audrey and Tex would not interrupt him. Ria needed his full attention. Georgetown was full of one-way streets. Why didn't they show them on the maps, Lee grumbled. Ria had made several illegal turns and headed the wrong way down an alley before she had spotted the Canary Street warehouses. He advised her to leave the car one block over with the keys inside. He didn't want to make it too hard for the FBI to recover their car.

Ria entered the warehouse as Lee monitored the video feed.

"Hello?" he heard her say. He didn't hear a response.

Ria panned the cavernous, dark space. In one corner were a desk, computer and phone. A small television sat on a crate. Several days' worth of fast-food wrappers littered the floor. Lee's stomach grumbled. He wished he hadn't skipped breakfast. But it was an operational necessity.

As Ria shuffled through the papers on the desk, an image came into focus. It was a list of news agencies with contact names and email addresses. To the side lay a press release cover page.

For Immediate Release.
Inside KU-BARK:
Is US Intelligence Exploiting
Children in the Name of National Security?

So it was true. Marvin's contact was going to expose their program, and he was ready to do it today. Audrey's hunch about KU-BARK had been correct. She had said MOLECHECK would neither confirm nor deny it, but here it was in black and white.

"See if you can find anything connecting Marvin to this guy," Lee squawked through Ria's earpiece.

"Great minds think alike," Ria said. The view from the camera was now of a wall, and all Lee could hear was the shuffling of papers.

The image suddenly jerked and blurred. Ria's charm bracelet clanked through the audio feed.

"What are you doing here?" It was a man's voice.

The image swirled again before coming into focus on a face. It was the man in Marvin's picture—Matthew Russell.

"I…I have an appointment. The Milbrook Group?" Ria was trying to sound cool, but Lee recognized the pitch as strained.

"You have the wrong place. Or do you?" Matthew Russell's face reappeared on the video stream

"Tom Milbrook, Milbrook Group? You're supposed to show me a warehouse property. 435 Canary?"

"What are you talking about?" Russell growled.

"Real estate. You're selling, my boss is interested in buying"

The shaking of the camera stopped.

"You've got the wrong place. Get out of here. You're on private property."

"Sorry, just following my boss's orders. I must have written the address wrong." Ria's heels click across the floor. The images were a blur, but she was heading for a circle of light. It must be the door. The light dimmed. Hannah appeared in the doorway, and then Marvin was pushed through.

He grew closer, the focal point moving from his face down to his knees. Ria's charm bracelet clattered hard, and the image blurred.

"Ria Santos," Hannah said. "You should have worked a little harder on your disguise. VIOLET would not be pleased. Your bracelet is a dead giveaway."

"What are you doing here?" Ria said. Lee couldn't tell what was happening. He heard a grunt, a screech and a thud. Then the image went dark, like the lens was pressed against something.

"Where do you know her from?" the man growled.

"She used to be on Kappa with us, but now she's on the goody-two-shoes team," Hannah said.

Images were blurring again. Lee's stomach lurched. They must be taking Ria back inside the warehouse.

"One of your brat friends stole something from me today, and I want it back," Matthew Russell hissed.

Lee heard the sound of something scrapping on wood. Ria hollered. "That's your problem. You're in big trouble if you think you can keep me here against my will. My team is watching all of this."

"What do you have?" The man demanded.

There were sounds of a struggle, and then the radio crackled.

"Damn. A radio. Hannah, tie her up. Marvin, make yourself useful for once." His voice grew louder. "Whoever is listening, you better do exactly as I say if you ever want to see this girl again. Bring me the thumb drive. Or else."

That was the last thing Lee heard.

The last thing he saw was a blur when the briefcase flipped over. When it settled, the lens was facing upward. Lee had a view of Ria's profile with the muzzle of a gun pointed right at her forehead.

Lee reached for the radio to switch frequencies. He had to alert Tex and Audrey. But before he could make the switch, the sound of footsteps pounded the hotel corridor.

— • — • • • — • • • — — • — — — — — • •

CONTROL convened the emergency meeting in her makeshift office at the Watergate. Lined up in front of her were MOLECHECK, VIOLET, DASH and FBI Agent Phillips. CONTROL was furious.

"What do you mean you've lost Alpha team?" she demanded from behind her desk.

FBI agent Phillips stood before the desk looked indignant, crossing his arms and resting them on his potbelly, the result of too many donuts during surveillance operations.

"We didn't lose them. They failed to show up at their agent meeting sites. But we caught many of the other recruits. Some of them were pretty funny when they realized the handcuffs were real and—"

"This is no joke." CONTROL slammed a file on the desk in front of her. "Find them and pick them up."

"We're not treating it as a joke. One of them stole my car," Agent Phillips growled.

"What kind of an operation are you running?" CONTROL stood and leaned across her desk toward Phillips. Her eyes flashed. "You saying the Bureau can't handle this?"

"I don't know if we have enough people to do a full search," Agent Phillips said, holding his ground. "I've got my best people on that other target."

"Call your headquarters and get more agents on the street. This is no longer a training exercise. We're going Code Red. Use force if necessary."

CONTROL's normally groomed hair was standing on end, and she looked like she was going to bite.

MOLECHECK stepped forward. Sweat ran down his bald spot into his red fuzz. His face was blotched red. "Do you think that's necessary? We're not sure this is a breach of national security. I know Alpha team. They're good kids."

"Not what I've seen of them." Agent Phillips turned abruptly and headed for the door. "I'll get a hundred agents out in the next five minutes. We'll use the training photos to ID them."

"Wait," CONTROL called out. "VIOLET, give him a list of the disguises you have issued to Alpha team. We can't let them slip away."

The Wrap-Up

Tex's watch beeped. It was noon. He was still hiding outside the warehouse, waiting for Marvin and his contact and trying to come up with a plan. He felt lower than a snake's belly. All he could think about was his agent meeting, which was supposed to be taking place at this exact moment on the path along the Potomac. His agent was bringing the names of the military officers leading the coup against the Ivanistan government. Tex leaned against the brick and kicked the gravel. He shoved his hands deeper into his pockets. Waiting was hard, but this was the real deal. Not Ivanistan. Still, with each passing minute, he felt his future slipping away. No one had gone in or left through the door during the last half hour. Ria wasn't responding to his radio calls. Neither was Lee. Nothing was happening.

A shuffling at the far end of the alley caught his attention. A man with gray hair sticking out of a baseball cap was headed straight for him. He wore a faded flannel shirt and carried a torn plastic bag. Tex tried to look casual. The guy would pass him soon, and he could get back to spying. But the old guy had other thoughts. He stopped right in front of Tex and then completed a perfect pirouette.

"It's me, silly."

"Aud?" Tex squinted at her. "Awesome disguise."

"Thanks," Audrey said, slightly out of breath. "It's not the one I was issued, but I figured since our mission has changed, I needed to mix it up. You know, blend in with the setting."

Tex smiled. She wasn't like the other girls. She was a true original, even if she was sometimes a little nutty. He could trust her with anything.

"What have you learned?" Audrey asked, looking around.

"A big fat nothing," Tex said. "I thought Marvin and his contact might come here after losing the flash drive, but I guess I was wrong. Like my pa says, just because a chicken has wings don't mean it can fly. I overestimated that weasel."

"Something else has gone wrong. Lee wasn't in his room, and I couldn't hand off the flash drive. But you wouldn't believe some of the stuff I found. I think I know who the practical joker is…"

"A gun, he's got a gun," Lee's voice burst in.

"What?" Tex asked, startled by the sudden return of radio transmissions.

"The FBI raided my room." Lee gasped. "I'm hiding in the housekeeper's closet. I need you guys, NOW! Ria's tied to a chair with a gun on her."

"Oh my gosh, oh my gosh, oh my gosh," Audrey squeaked.

"Who's got the gun?" Tex was totally confused.

"It's the man from the photograph. NIGHT-WIND's there too. Ah, got to go…"

"LAB-MAN! What's happening?" Tex was met with radio silence. He tried to ignore the burn he was feeling in his gut. The door to the warehouse was in clear view. No one had gone in or out since he had been there. "How'd they get past me?" Tex said.

"There's got to be another entrance," Audrey said.

"I'm going in." Tex darted to the warehouse door and cracked it open. He couldn't see a thing. He kicked the door open. "Oh man, it's a fake." A wall of bricks sealed the entrance. "I've been burning daylight outside a dead end this whole time?"

"It's got to be around back," Audrey said.

The old man version of Audrey sprinted around the warehouse and past an ice cream truck that was blocking the alley.

Tex pulled Audrey down by the back door and looked over his shoulder. "I thought I saw something move." Probably a cat, even though the flash was too white for a cat. "Wait a minute. Why did Lee say Hannah and the contact were in there, but he didn't mention Marvin?"

"Marvin called the man *Dad* on the boat. He also did something really odd, I think he tried to help me," Audrey said.

"The contact is his dad? Why is Hannah in there? Is he holding her hostage too?"

"I know you're going to think I'm crazy, but I've had a weird feeling about Hannah the past few days. I don't think she can be trusted."

"And Marvin?"

"Marvin's complicated," Audrey said.

Tex cracked the door open. He could see figures moving back and forth.

"You think that stealing the thumb drive will stop me," the man said. Tex knew he had to be Matthew Russell. He had the face of a sheep-killing dog. "I have enough information provided by my bumbling son."

"No one will believe you," Ria shouted.

"Watch." Russell said. He walked over to a computer and started to type with one hand while keeping the gun pointed at Ria. "The names, addresses and parents of the current class of Junior Spies will soon be leaked to all the major newspapers in America."

Tex picked up a broken brick. "Do you think you can go in there and cause some chaos? I have an idea."

"I can do chaos."

He weighed the brick fragment in his hand. He still had the rope he had taken off the mule. Moving quickly, he unraveled the end so he had four strands and found a second brick fragment. He tied two strands around each piece and swung it a few times to get a feel for the movement. An improvised bola like one of the ranch hands had taught him to use to catch runaways.

"You be careful," Tex said. "A dead snake can still bite."

"Spies can't be timid," Audrey said. She rushed the door.

"They're after me!" she screamed. "Get 'em off of me!"

Audrey beat her clothing with her hands, screaming that invisible bugs were attacking her. The distraction worked. Matthew Russell stopped typing and stepped in Audrey's direction. No one noticed Tex as he slid in along the wall. Swinging the bola, he aimed. He had one shot. He released the rope. The bricks soared through the air and found its mark: Matthew Russell. When it wrapped around Russell's outstretched arm, the bricks knocked the gun from his hand and sent him to the ground. The gun hit the floor and skidded, stopping a few feet in front of Audrey. She just stood there.

"Grab it, Aud," Tex yelled as he headed toward Russell.

Audrey was like a cat, pouncing on it while Hannah Martin tried to block her. Marvin landed on top of Hannah and grabbed her hair, pulling it tight.

Tex faked a move around Russell and dove for the computer. He yanked out the power cord and pressed the delete key.

"Get off of me you reject," Hannah screamed.

Russell hit Tex in the side of the head with one of the bricks and grabbed for the laptop on the desk. A splitting pain shot through Tex's head, blurring his vision. Somehow he kept his finger pressed on the delete key and watched the last of the message disappear.

"Nobody move!" came a voice from behind. Tex turned enough to see Eric Little, the camp counselor, with a gun in his hand. He wore bright white tennis shoes. Tex knew immediately that was the flash of white he had seen earlier. Matthew Russell moved too, twisting one of Tex's arms behind him, before locking his other arm around Tex's neck. Tex gasped for air as Audrey struggled with Hannah. She gave the gun a swift kick, and it slid across the floor, coming to a stop under Eric Little's foot.

"Back away." Eric pointed to Audrey, Hannah and Marvin.

Audrey sputtered. "Y-y-you traitor. I knew you were involved—"

"Don't move or I'll kill the kid," Matthew Russell commanded.

Tex stopped struggling when he felt his shoulder pop under the pressure. The pain seared hotter than blue blazes. This was bad. Real bad.

From then on, things happened so fast Tex had trouble later recalling them. The sound of a gun going off ripped through the empty warehouse. Matthew Russell loosened his grip on Tex. Tex dropped to the ground in an evasive move. Russell was on the ground next to him, but not moving. But something was odd. Tex tried to slow the thoughts screaming through his brain. The sound. It wasn't a normal 9 mm round. It wasn't a crack, but more like a ka-thud. It sounded like a dart, like the kind his pa used to tag cattle, knocking them out for a little while.

Eric untied Ria, grabbing the papers and the laptop from the desk.

"Follow me," he said to the surprised recruits. "The FBI is on the way to clean up the mess." He gestured toward Matthew Russell, who lay motionless on the floor.

Tex stuck his leg out tripping Hannah when she tried to run for it. Eric slapped cuffs on one of her arms and the other on Marvin and dragged them to a waiting truck blocking the alley. Tex, Ria and Audrey followed. Tex gripped his shoulder. With each step the pain stung meaner than a mama wasp. Painted on the side of the van was "Igloo Ice Cream & More." The rear doors opened as they approached. Inside, there was no ice cream, but metal shelves stacked with electronic equipment. Two technicians sat in front of monitors with headphones. Tex knew right away they were inside a mobile surveillance platform. Eric handcuffed Hannah to the armrest and Marvin next to her before crawling up front, next to the driver. The truck peeled out of the alley. They headed east.

For five miserable minutes Tex and the others listened to Hannah protest this was a violation of her rights. Her father was an important elected official, and they would be hearing from him. She was innocent and demanded to be released. Tex threatened to put a piece of duct tape over her mouth if she didn't pipe down. On one of the van monitors, the team watched while the FBI raided the warehouse, arresting Matthew Russell.

"Were you really going to expose the program?" Audrey asked Marvin.

"I didn't want to. I wanted my dad to like me, to want to be with me."

"I can't believe I ever considered you my friend." Ria's curls flew as she stabbed her finger in the air at Hannah.

The van squealed to a stop underneath the Watergate. "This is where the three of you get out." Eric pointed at Audrey, Tex and Ria.

Lee stood on the dock, hands behind his back in cuffs, two security escorts at his side. If things weren't looking so serious and his shoulder didn't hurt so much, Tex would have laughed. With his rumpled button-down shirt and long face, Lee looked more like a lost puppy than a criminal.

"What happened to you...?" Tex started to ask Lee, when two beefy security officers grabbed Tex by his collar and frog-marched him fast as all get out toward the hotel elevators. He was informed he had ten minutes to pack his stuff and was forbidden to talk to anybody. Before entering the elevator, a security officer grabbed Tex's arm and popped the dislocated shoulder back in place, ignoring Tex's yelp.

By the time Tex returned to the loading dock, Hannah, Marvin and the ice cream truck were gone. Lee was waiting in the van the instructors had taken from camp, cuffed to the armrest. As soon as Ria and Audrey boarded, the van left. No one said a word during the trip back to camp. What was there to talk about? Tex knew they were all about to be eliminated.

The Murder Board

Lee sat with the others in their spy school homeroom; relieved that the silent treatment was about to end. For the past two days, they had been denied entry to the spy school facilities, except to write reports on their individual actions. Everywhere they went, Security followed. CONTROL no longer relied on the hidden cameras and microphones. Alpha team was a security threat. Lee felt they should be wearing a big loser sign instead.

Audrey, dark circles under her eyes, was doodling the day's date on an index card. Lee recognized the numbers; they were the same ones Audrey claimed were her lucky numbers. Ria slumped in her chair, her face completely hidden behind a screen of curls. Tex was making paper airplanes out of water-soluble paper. The bag of M&Ms Tex had given to him sat on the ops table, unopened. Lee couldn't eat. They were doomed.

"ATTEN-TION!" DUTCH bellowed as the door burst open. Alpha team jumped to their feet.

"Be seated. CONTROL has asked me to fill in for MOLECHECK. UNDERSTOOD?" Dressed in his standard camouflage fatigues, DUTCH paced in front of the ops table studying each recruit. The only other time Lee had ever seen him, they had been outside. Somehow he looked even bigger and more dangerous when confined to a small classroom. Like he could kill you with his pinky.

"I've been asked to review the exercise and do the final debrief. Eyes forward!"

An image of tanks rolling through empty streets filled the whiteboard at the front of the room.

"Over the past few days, the coup plotted by the military went into its final stages. Your team had an opportunity to stop it, if you had met with your agents and obtained the intelligence. COW-BOY, your agent would have given you the names of the military officers heading the plot. LAB-MAN, your agent would have told you when the military planned to launch the attack on the Prime Minister's residence."

Lee hung his head.

"Your opportunity to break the agreement between the coup leaders and the labor unions was lost when MIND-READER didn't show for her meeting with STRIKER and his uncle Frederick Lavinski, the head of the unions. I could go on, but the point is the coup has happened. The Prime Minister was shot by firing squad this morning after a military tribunal convicted him of high treason. The labor union demonstrations are out of control. There are riots in the city center. Reports of a new power struggle emerging between the Labor leaders and the coup leaders..."

While DUTCH briefed them on the dismal turn of events in Ivanistan, Lee sank lower in his chair. It was hard to remember this was just a scenario. They had lived the live problem for the entire summer.

DUTCH passed out the individual instructor evaluations for the final exercise. It was F's all around.

Lee had never received an F. He was thankful his parents would not find out. He had worried about how he could keep spying secret. But now, there was nothing to tell. He wasn't going to be a spy. He could pretend spy camp hadn't happened.

When MOLECHECK and CONTROL entered the room Lee felt his stomach tighten. MOLECHECK was wearing a black tie with a white scythe on it; the kind executioners carry. He was pretty sure his teammates felt just as panicked.

Without a word, MOLECHECK distributed large white envelopes, each stamped "Top Secret" and bearing the recruits' codenames.

MOLECHECK and DUTCH walked to the back of the class, leaving CONTROL front and center. "The Murder Board has finished its deliberations. While you do not have a need-to-know about most of our discussions, I think you should know about the investigations."

Ria squirmed in her chair. "I gave 'em back their car," she grumbled.

"Security was aware we had a breach early on," CONTROL said. "One of the recruits was determined to be an imposter."

CONTROL pulled out an 8" x 10" photograph. "The young lady claiming to be Hannah Martin, codename NIGHT-WIND, is in fact not Hannah Martin. She is actually Gina Fink. Ms. Fink's father is a congressman looking for a way to shut down the program. He found a way in through Matthew Russell. Matthew was an early wash out of the Junior Spy program over twenty years ago, and has a chip on his shoulder. Russell is actually…"

"Marvin's dad," Audrey said.

"Yes," CONTROL continued. "We'd picked up some intelligence he was trying to penetrate the camp. So we brought BULLDOG in on a counterintelligence mission to trap NIGHT-WIND and to identify her accomplice. Marvin lives in Oregon with his mother and stepfather. We hadn't made the connection because Marvin used his stepfather's last name. We now know that Marvin hadn't had contact with his real father, since Russell walked out on them eight years ago. EAGLE-EYES was not on our radar. We were so focused on NIGHT-WIND and MIND-READER."

"Why me?" Audrey squeaked.

"Let's just say you exhibited several odd behaviors that made us question your loyalty. From meeting with the subjects after curfew to leaving personal items in areas of the camp that were off-limits." Control held up a round, blue object studded with fake jewels.

"You found my compact?" Audrey said.

"Yes, blocking the view of a security camera. Very clever I might add."

"I dropped it in the woods during my agent meeting with BULLDOG. How do you know he didn't take it?"

"Because Eric was working for us. We used him as a dangle, giving Hannah the impression he was unhappy with the program and could be turned. But she didn't bite; even after we let it leak he had been recalled because of a failed mission. BULLDOG was unable to catch NIGHT-WIND because EAGLE-EYES was doing most of the legwork; collecting intelligence and maintaining contact with Russell. NIGHT-WIND was the brains behind the operation."

"This explains everything." Audrey eyes widened.

"But why would Hannah betray me...us," Ria asked, brows furrowed. "She was my friend."

"The Congressman and Hannah a.k.a Gina have fooled a lot of people. They are both good at manipulating people by doing favors. Why? Greed. Power. Control."

Lee watched Ria's face. He saw a storm brewing. Ria did not like being wrong.

"We set up a sting for the final exercise, planning to catch NIGHT-WIND in the act, but Alpha team decided to interfere in an official investigation, also a crime, I note."

Interfered? Lee had felt like a real spy. Now he felt like an imposter.

Without warning, Ria exploded out of her chair, her hair careening in dangerous directions.

"We did it for a reason. We knew EAGLE-EYES was trying to blow the cover of the Junior Spy Program." She started with a laundry list of Marvin's odd behavior during training. "We needed evidence to back up our theories. We may have made the wrong decision not to tell you or MOLECHECK, but we decided catching the mole was more important than passing the final exam."

To Lee's amazement, Tex rose and stood next to Ria. "Ria is telling the truth. We thought we had the mole identified. We didn't realize we were interfering in an official investigation. You can hang your hat on it. If anyone should be held responsible, it should be me. I talked all of them into catching Marvin. And Ria, you should certify her. She got mixed up with us at the end."

Ria turned toward Tex, her eyes blazing.

Oh Einstein. Here comes another chemical explosion. Lee sunk down in his chair.

"Hero-boy may think he talked us into it, but I supported everything we did. It's the truth, and you should know it."

Lee didn't know who had surprised him more. Tex or Ria. MOLECHECK had told them a hundred times they should not shy away from speaking truth to power. But Tex standing up for Ria?

It was CONTROL who stunned them all. She smiled. "Well done. But PUZZLE-GIRL, you missed one crucial element. Alpha team targeted the real mole. Without your work, both of them would have slipped through our fingers, and the program would have been exposed."

MOLECHECK handed each of them an envelope. "Inside, you'll find the critiques of your ops planning, and site and intelligence reports on your mole catching operation. I was very impressed, as was the Murder Board. 'Truly professional' was their comment. I particularly liked the way you did this on your own initiative. Well done. Any questions?"

"Why did you lie about the codename?" Audrey asked MOLECHECK.

"KU-BARK is not the current codename. We changed it after Russell exposed it.

"What happens to Hannah and Marvin?" Ria said.

"Hannah has been charged with conspiracy to expose classified information. We are certain her father will tie this one up in the courts for several years. Marvin is a little trickier. We believe his father coerced him. He's agreed to testify in exchange for a lighter sentence," MOLECHECK said. "He was good at casting suspicion on others. We found his prints on the stolen soda can concealment device he tried to frame Tex with, but we believe Hannah, not Marvin, planted Audrey's compact in the computer room after accessing the training files."

"So Marvin wasn't good, but he wasn't all bad either," Audrey said.

"Never underestimate the enemy," MOLECHECK said.

"That brings me back to the Murder Board," CONTROL said. Lee had almost forgotten the Murder Board, and the fact they had failed the final exercise.

"The decision is final. There is no appeal process."

CONTROL sat on the edge of MOLECHECK's desk, saying nothing for what felt to Lee like a lifetime.

"MOLECHECK argued on your behalf that this was an unusual case."

Lee looked at MOLECHECK, whose lip curled in a half grin. He looked like the cat that ate the canary.

"The board has decided Alpha team showed exceptional judgment and dedication to the mission. Your team observed and acted on information other teams missed. You have been cleared of all charges."

It was what came next that floored Lee.

"You four are the only recruits to be certified as Junior Spies."

Joy burst through Lee like a supersize package of Starbursts. He couldn't wait to tell his brothers. And his dad. But what if his dad didn't approve? What if he couldn't tell anyone? Who'd believe him anyway?

Tex crushed him in a bear hug and Audrey and Ria piled on. He didn't need anyone else to believe in him. His team did.

— • — • • • — • • • — — • — — — — • •

Memo for the Record
Date/Time: 11 AUG/1600Z
To: CONTROL
From: Director of Intel Center
Re: Alpha team

POTUS in PERIL. Request immediate deployment of Alpha team. Retired agents Alfred Wong, Marlena Rochais, Carmen Santos, and Jed Shaker already notified of certification and movement to operational status of their children.

Coincidence is an everyday occurrence for Audrey. Signs appear out of nowhere, and her senses guide her in dealing with others. It is as if she can read minds.

A medallion from her grandmamma, helps Audrey channel her inner strength when she feels the pressure, often surprising herself and others.

Audrey Rochais
MIND-READER

At the age of four, Lee took apart his parent's vacuum cleaner, and reassembled it with a discarded computer chip to create the world's first self-propelled vacuum.

Lee's dream is to push the limits of technology and imagination creating one-of-a-kind gadgets for his team.

Lee Wong
LAB-MAN

At age six, Ria found a flaw in the New York Times Sunday crossword puzzle and sent a corrected version to an embarrassed Will Shortz.

Her determination to figure out the most difficult problems make her an enigma as well as a source of constant conflict with those in her sight lines.

Ria Santos
PUZZLE-GIRL

A risk taker from a very young age, Tex never met a rule he couldn't break, or at least bend.

He is determined to be the first at everything and hides his real feelings behind a cover of always pushing for the next challenge or adventure.

Tex Shaker
COW-BOY

Spy-Speak Glossary

Agent	A spy.
Alias	A fake name spies use when conducting espionage missions.
All-clear signal	A visual signal to indicate that there is no danger.
Assessment	Interpretation or analysis of information; a stage of the intelligence cycle.
Biometrics	An identification system that uses unique traits and characteristics to identify a person (fingerprints, DNA, odor, etc.)
Briefing	Presentation of intelligence information.
Bug	A listening device.
Bug-out kit	A traveling pack that spies use to hold their spy equipment.
Brush pass	A form of communication in which something is discretely passed between two people as they walk past each other, giving no indication that they know each other.
Casing assignment	A mission to precisely describe a place that will be used for spy activities.
Choke points	A point of congestion or blockage.
Classified	Secret.
Cloak and dagger	Secrecy surrounding clandestine intelligence operations.
Code	A system of disguising messages.
Codename	A name spies use to protect their identity.

Collection	Gathering of intelligence; a stage of the intelligence cycle.
Communications (Commo)	Secret systems spies use to talk to each other.
Communications Intelligence (COMINT)	Intelligence picked up from listening to phone or radio conversations
Compromise	Exposure of a secret operation.
Concealment device	A container used to hide stuff.
Cover	A fake story used to hide espionage activities.
Crypt	A word used as a substitute for another word or name to hide the meaning of the word or name.
Dead drop	A form of communication where a package is left for a spy to pick up later, avoiding a personal meeting of spies.
Debriefing	A meeting during which intelligence is obtained.
Deception	An operation meant to confuse or deceive someone.
Decode	Return a coded message to plain text that can be read and understood.
Decrypt	Decode.
Deploy	To move to a different location to start a new mission.
Disguise	Something that changes one's appearance.
Dissemination	Sending out an intelligence report; a stage in the intelligence cycle.
Diversion	An operation that is designed to draw attention as a way to permit another operation to take place unnoticed.

Elicitation	The art of getting information without asking direct questions.
Encryption	Putting plain text messages into code.
Espionage	Spying.
Exfiltration	Secret departure after the mission is complete.
Human Intelligence (HUMINT)	Intelligence collected by humans through agent meetings or contacts.
Impersonal communication	Communication methods with spies that are done without personal, direct contact.
Intelligence	Secret information of national security interest.
(Intel) Intelligence Cycle	The espionage process of issuing requirements, collecting, analyzing, and disseminating intelligence.
Invisible ink	Ink that is not always visible to the naked eye.
Legend	A false identity and cover story.
Microdots	Secret writing in the form of microscopic messages that look like dots.
Mission	Intelligence operation.
Mole	A double agent.
Need-to-know	The principle for limited access to intelligence.
Operations (Ops)	Spy activities.
Optical reader	An electronic eye used to scan documents or other items.
Parole	Secret code word exchange.
Rabbit	Target person being surveilled.

Raw intelligence	Facts, not analysis.
Recognition signal	A secret signal meant to help spies identify each other.
Recruiting	Asking someone to become a spy.
Recruitment cycle	The stages of how agents are found and managed: spotting/assessing, development, recruitment, handling, termination
Requirements	Questions that direct spies on what intelligence to seek or activities to take; a stage in the intelligence cycle.
Safe house	A house or apartment where secret meetings are held.
Secret writing	Techniques spies use to hide written messages.
Signal	A secret sign spies use to send messages.
Sleuthing	Spying.
Spy	A secret agent.
Surveillance	Monitoring someone's movements secretly.
Target	The focus of an intelligence operation.
Tradecraft	The art of espionage or how spies work secretly.
Zulu time	Coordinated Universal Time. Eastern Standard Time is Zulu time minus 5 hours

About the Authors

Melissa Mahle is a former CIA Intelligence officer, a.k.a. a spy. She was one of a handful of female operations officers fluent in Arabic, working in the Middle East to keep Americans safe.

Since leaving the CIA in 2002, Melissa has embarked on a new career as an author, Hollywood film advisor and media commentator. Her first book was, *Denial and Deception: An Insider's View of the CIA from Iran-Contra to 9/11*, Nation Books, 2005.

Melissa is active in youth programs at the International Spy Museum in Washington D.C. and has consulted on several spy thrillers. Her recent film credits include *Salt*, starring Angelina Jolie, and *Hanna* with Saoirse Roman and Cate Blanchett. Melissa was featured in the documentary *Secrecy*, which opened at the Sundance Film Festival in 2008.

Kathryn Dennis began her career in New York as an advertising art director where she first started putting words and pictures together.

After completing the fiction-writing program at the University of Washington, a chance workshop at Hugo House started her journey of writing for children.

She won the 2006 Society of Children's Book Writers and Illustrators Kimberly Colen Grant for a picture book.